A War
in
The Bronx

ISBN-13: 978-0-9972920-7-7
ISBN-10: 0-9972920-7-5

First printing: April 2017

Cover design by ThomasMax

Published by:

ThomasMax Publishing
P.O. Box 250054
Atlanta, GA 30325
www.thomasmax.com

A War
in The Bronx

A. Shane Etter

ThomasMax
Your Publisher
For The 21st Century

ACKNOWLEDGMENTS

First I'd like to thank, from the bottom of my heart, my mentor, two-time Pulitzer nominee, Jedwin Smith. This is number three with your help and it keeps getting better. Thank you.

Jedwin introduced me to a great editor, Chuck Clark. Thank you for your magic, Chuck.

Thank you to the members of our ongoing Writer's Workshop. You challenge me and make me better. Although I don't always show it, I appreciate it.

To my sister, Amy Mills and my brother, CW5 U.S. Army, (Ret.), Kevin Etter, thank you for a lifetime of love and support.

Thanks to all my friends, old and new, writers and non-writers, who have supported me in words and actions. I will always be grateful.

And thank you to all of the great writers I read, for inspiring me and helping me, even if you don't know you're doing it.

Last, but not least, thank you Lee Clevenger of Thomas Max Publishing, for believing in "War."

Part One
Bronx Streets

Chapter One
The Neighborhood

Detective Second-Grade John Maloney had his ever–present copy of the *Daily News* clenched under his arm as he strode along Simpson Street toward the front doors of the precinct made famous in film and literature as Fort Apache, The Bronx, written by the great novelist, screen writer and Hollywood director, Heywood Gould. Maloney's pace told anyone watching he was on a mission, head down, hands in his overcoat pockets, the collar of the coat turned up against the early morning chill.

Pregnant gray clouds were threatening to dump a miserable load of snow on the city. Some people walked slowly in the cold; the near-freezing temperatures making it too painful to rush. In truth, the cold made Maloney move faster. With his quick pace, even in the frigid early morning weather, he'd worked up a light sweat. He was a New Yorker to his bones. As Mayor Ed Koch once said, New Yorkers walk faster, talk faster, think faster. Even through the thick skin of his cheek the chill pained the bad molar Maloney needed to have filled. He'd have to call his dentist—the one he'd seen since he was a kid. The man was still in the same Central Park East office Johnny had visited as a child.

The coat he wore was a knock-off, a copy of a Burberry, khaki colored with camel-check tartan plaid lining. He couldn't afford the genuine article on a New York City police detective's salary. And fortunately with his average build he didn't require an even more expensive bespoke version which was way out of the question. With his dark hair, untouched by gray as it was, and everyman size, if anyone were paying attention they'd think he were ten years younger than his actual thirty-five. And almost pretty. They'd never suspect he was an NYPD veteran detective of ten years. He told himself the mustache he cultivated was just to make him look less like a kid, a young, overly pretty kid. The other detectives gave him too much shit about his looks. And women wished he were single.

The nine-foot-tall double doors creaked noisily, divulging their age, as he strained to open one against the wind. The once-beautiful wood entrance, entering the home of all Bronx detectives, was stained with the grime, dirt, soot and exhaust from decades in the elements and rough to the touch from the filth.

The desk sergeant greeted him with a make-believe scowl from behind his aerie, the immense elevated desk overlooking everything and everyone on his watch.

"Good morning, Sergeant Cabrera," Maloney greeted loudly, feigning enthusiasm that he didn't mean and that didn't fool the sergeant.

"Morning, Maloney—what're you grinning about?"

"Not grinning, Sergeant. Just happy to be here."

"Well, your buddy Musso's turning over a new leaf, got in early. Get in there and hit the streets."

"Yes, Sergeant."

Detective First-Grade Carmine Musso, the senior detective in their partnership, wore the scowl that was his constant companion, that gave him a permanently pissed-off look. Even so, he had plenty of friends on the job. Most liked him. The longest serving detective, he was an institution at Fort Apache. Entering reports from the previous shift, behind his partition in the squad room, he could usually get the paperwork done while downing two cups of Joe. Back in the early days, the only task that might have driven Musso to forsake law enforcement was the paperwork. But he toughed it out even though, because he was somewhat of a rebel, his first thought was to tell them to take the job and shove it where there was never any sunshine. Everything a detective did had to be documented and after thirty years on the job he was plenty tired of it. Musso had once been hard but now with age was turning to soft. He still had a lot of muscle, but it was cushioned with a layer of fat; a five o'clock shadow by the time he arrived at work. He was pushing sixty and with his ever-expanding middle and black hair graying at the temples—Maloney had watched the gray form through the years—resembled the aging boxer, Jake LaMotta, or at least Robert DeNiro's film portrayal of him in *Raging Bull,* the movie about the Italian fighter's life. Coincidental not only because of his Italian looks but because Musso had been a boxer in his younger days—Golden Gloves and the New York Police Athletic League. He'd always thought with the right manager, or trainer, he could have contended for the championship, but such were the dreams of aging former high school athletes the world over. It was also the reason he carried the sobriquet he took pride in—Rocky.

Maloney leaned against Musso's desk.

"About time you showed up. Damn, you get later every day. When I was your age I always got in early. One question, did you bring lunch with you?" Musso spoke around the round white lollipop stick protruding from his mouth.

"Who do you think you are—Jerry Seinfeld?" They both wielded a south Bronx accent though Maloney's, a little more polished due to his Columbia University education, not as mouthy as Musso's.

"Jackie Mason is more of my generation." In truth he really wasn't old enough to remember watching the comedian on television, but references like that helped him with the crusty old curmudgeon image he coveted.

"Smartass."

Musso withdrew the partially wounded sucker stick and peered at it as if to study it. "You know, I had forgotten how good these were. I picked up a handful at the barbershop yesterday. I hadn't had one since I was a kid.

"You aren't supposed to grab a handful, Rocky. One per visit."

"He's been cutting my hair twice a month for over ten years and I've never gotten even one before so he's still ahead of the game."

"Whatever. Let me do my morning business. Give me fifteen with the Daily News and I'll be ready to go."

"Man, eat some bran muffins. It shouldn't take you more than five."

"Yeah, yeah, yeah. Like you know my bowel movements better than I do."

"I know you're full of shit."

"Oh, that's rich, Rock. You been taking lessons from Jackie Mason?"

"I think he's dead. If he isn't, he should be."

"Oughta be. I'll be back in fifteen."

Five minutes later Maloney came running back to the squad room waving The Daily News, shouting."You're not going to believe it."

"What? What ain't I gonna believe?"

"Trudy, Trudy Dylan disappeared on a hike in the mountains and is presumed dead."

"Get the fuck outta here."

The Daily News had picked it up on the wire from Atlanta Journal and Constitution, recognized and respected all over the south as the AJC, and small weekly papers in north GA.

"No, it's right here in the News. You know it still favors Trudy for helping us bust open the Cloisters murder case."

"Lemme see."

Maloney gave Musso the morning edition and he popped it loudly before spreading it out on his desk. Then, he retrieved his readers, his one crutch against creeping age, from the oversize yellow bowl-shaped coffee mug adorned with a smiley-face, his daughter had given him one Christmas when she was a child, before attempting to digest the news. Someone once said that fifty was either the old age of youth or the youth of old age. Musso was halfway through that decade and would not go quietly into the Dylan Thomas night. Maloney stood above him and re-read the article from over Musso's shoulder.

Patrick, Trudy and their detective agency partner, Jeff Byrd, had been hiking on the north Georgia portion of The Trail of Tears when Trudy went over a cliff. Animals got to the body before Dylan and Byrd could.

Shaking his head, Musso said, "The Bronx streets are tough but I'll take our manmade canyons and the animals on our streets over stone canyons and the four–legged wild ones, any day."

"No shit. You got that right. Can you imagine going up against a bear, or a wolf? Wolves are predatory animals and they would eat our yankee New York asses up. We need to call Patrick. I've still got his number here." Maloney pulled out his cellphone and scrolled down to Patrick's number. Touched the number and after a moment: "Patrick Dylan's phone."

"This is Detective Johnny Maloney. New York Homicide."

"Yes detective, I remember you. Jeff Byrd here." Maloney recognized Byrd's deep baritone.

Maloney switched on the phone's speaker function and laid it flat in the center of Musso's desk.

"Nice to talk you again. I'm here with my partner Carmine Musso. You remember him. We just heard about Trudy and wanted to check on Paddy." They'd met Byrd in the abandoned subway tunnels underneath Manhattan just a few weeks before. A harrowing experience none of them would soon forget. Musso grunted hello.

"Good to talk to you again, except for the reason. I assumed you guys had heard what happened and I know you're both aware of what's involved in what's been going on here, so I can let you know what really happened. Trudy was kidnapped by Indians ghosts controlled by mutants, and they killed her. The newspaper accounts were a load of shit we fed them."

"Indian ghosts and mutants? Huh…that I can believe." Musso could accept almost anything after almost thirty years on the job in New York City and after killing one of the mutants underneath Manhattan with Patrick and Trudy. "Man, I'm getting tired of all this supernatural shit."

"No kidding. But how's Paddy holding up?" Maloney was concerned about their friend now.

"Ah, you know. Not good, but as soon as the service is over he'll be out for blood— mutant, vampire, zombie, or any other kind he can find.

Musso said, "Maybe we can help with that."

Maloney could read his partner's mind, even better than the mutants could and he knew what he was thinking and agreed. "Yeah, we'll go back underground, see if we can stir up anything." They both recalled the mutant creature they'd encountered and killed in a sewage pool underneath Manhattan.

They exchanged good wishes and agreed to stay in touch.

***

Walking to the city-owned lot to retrieve their dark blue unmarked Crown Vic from its regular spot, their mood was severely dampened by the news.

"Poor Paddy," Maloney said.

"Poor mutants, I say," said Carmine. "Patrick will be out for blood."

"I hope so," Johnny agreed. "I can't imagine how he must feel."

"Definitely."

"Just think if it were one of our wives."

"No kidding. Speaking of wives, how is Mary Catherine?"

"Good, She's good. Happy as a lark since she got to go to a Broadway play with some of her besties this past weekend. And I got her a room at the Marriott Marquis in Times Square so they wouldn't have to worry about getting home late. She said some big-shot celebrity was staying on the twenty-third floor—she didn't know who—but whoever it was reserved every room on the floor for their entourage.

Musso said, "Probably some Third world billionaire oil sheik."

"Maybe. Anyways, her room came with a free breakfast, and none of that continental shit—a full hot breakfast from the lobby restaurant. The whole thing cost me an arm and a leg, but at least it kept her from dragging my ass along, and she'd been talking about going to Atlantic City. AC, shit that would have really cost me. So it was the least of two evils." He shook his head at the thought. "All in all, it wasn't that bad. They saw *Romeo and Juliet* with—who was it? Shit. I don't know from actors. That Hollywood hottie they called him—oh yeah, Orlando Bloom, that's it. I *do* remember him from *Lord Of The Rings*. He played Legolas. Pretty good action flick. Anyways, she said when he took his shirt off, all the women in the audience just about lost their shit. They were on sixth-row center stage. Said his abs were like razors."

"That's what the girls used to say about me."

"Yeah, yeah, yeah. Anyway, let's go see if we can roust some of those dealers over on Valentine."

"Good, great, that'd be a good way to start the week. Valentine Avenue reminds me of Washington Heights at its worst, back in the day—sheesh."

"You know, you really have some great stories from back then. You should oughta write a book."

"Like I know from writing."

"You could get someone—a real author—to write it. You tell him the stories and he'd put them down on paper."

"That might not be a bad idea. Maybe I could be the next Joseph Wambaugh, or Serpico. I'll have to think about it."

"Don't get carried away, Rock. Wait, wait, maybe you oughta write about some of our cases, and when they make a movie from it, Nicholas Cage could play me."

"Now, who's getting carried away?"

"Yeah, you're right. Cage is too old to play me. He could probably play you, though. Nah, that won't work. He's too skinny to play you. Nobody would believe that. He'd have to put on at least a hundred pounds, give or take."

"Yeah, sure he would."

As they walked, they passed the fenced-in concrete yards and compounds of the two-story attached homes that lined the streets. Neighborhood kids had an early-morning stickball game going on. Almost every house had a basketball goal planted in the paved over yard. Former NBA greats Jamal Mashburn, Dick McGuire, and Nate "Tiny" Archibald, among others, had honed their craft on these homegrown courts in the Bronx.

"Leave your sister alone," came a mother's shout from a second-story window. Three boys, used to being guilty, froze.

Mid-November was an interesting time in the neighborhood. A smattering of Halloween decorations refused to surrender territory, but Christmas decorations were gaining a foothold. An assortment of inflatable Santas, Peanuts characters and Disney favorites in the yards and on the roofs kept vigil over the neighborhoods.

The elevated train provided a noisy backdrop to a UN delegation of different languages: Puerto Rican, Cuban, Jamaican, Chinese and if, like Musso, you knew where to listen, even English. The first immigrants to the Bronx were Irish, Italians and Jews. Blue collar families; they were tailors, shopkeepers, bridge- and skyscraper-builders and restaurateurs. And cops. Don't forget the cops. The newest generation was various offerings of Latinos, Middle Easterners and Asians, all of them salt-of-the-earth types, and like their predecessors, hard working people who only wanted to make a home, in which to watch their children grow up, have grandchildren and to make a better life than they could ever hope to have in their native lands.

A Chinese laundry offered the warm sweet smell of laundry detergent and fabric softener blowing from the double glass-front doors. The warm aroma a counterpoint to the early season, biting cold of mid-November, unusual even for New York.

Chapter Two
The Present and the Past

Rev was the king of the Bronx drug trade. James Washington carried that unlikely nickname because he was a preacher's son, considered becoming a preacher himself. However, he couldn't get over the resentment he felt for his father for, as he thought, putting his flock first, before his own family. As a child he started out playing Pop Warner, then middle school and growing to Six-foot-four and 220 pounds, Rev had been an all-city wide receiver in high school. Won him looks from a number of universities to play football, but his grades were good enough to get him accepted at the city's own Ivy League school, Columbia University. Rev was even smart enough to have earned a degree had he not started using drugs. Only marijuana and a little blow, but although he abandoned the pursuit of his degree, even then his innate intelligence won out over the illegal habit. Helped him to figure out that if getting his next high could cause him to throw away his education, and a shot at a career in professional football with the requisite seven-figure income, then he knew that drugs would be good business. Knew that people would pay huge amounts for the high drugs gave them. He started as a low level street corner businessman, but with his cunning and intelligence—and after kicking some other dealers' asses—he soon had a platoon of runners, kids, working for him and was supplying the local public schools. It wasn't a big leap from there to supplying the entire Bronx and men and women from all over the country coming up from Manhattan when they visited the city for business.

Rev's organization was now generating more than a hundred million a year in revenue through the sale of cocaine, heroin and weed and with that kind of money he'd put together an organization—the Zombies—of street-corner dealers, runners, accountants, legal advisors and his inner circle of business advisors. The smartest thing he'd done was to insulate himself from everyone involved except for his inner circle. Rev was practically a ghost, a myth. No one except for the close group knew what he looked like or even if he really existed. His personal income was over a million dollars a month tax-free He lived in a north Bronx mansion and only kept the boarded-up crumbling brownstone on Valentine because it remained ground zero for his continuously growing empire. But its interior—filled with classic furniture, antiques, accessories and surprising appointments— belied its ramshackle exterior. He also kept it as a storage place, a warehouse, for a short-term supply, a month's worth of drugs. He couldn't allow the Zombies to run low but he also couldn't store any at his North Bronx mansion. Too far from his customers and also too risky. He couldn't be caught with illegal merch at his home. And there were always guards at the Valentine Street headquarters.

Rev's success made him a target of rival organizations: the Russians, Chinese, the Romanians, other African-Americans, New York City cops and the Feds. Thus far he'd been smart and lucky.

His biggest worry was that someone close to him would get arrested and, to save his sorry ass, would cooperate with law enforcement. But because no one but his four closest advisors, all friends since college or even earlier, actually knew him, and he knew they would never betray him, he felt like he was as safe as possible in the world he'd chosen.

***

Musso and Maloney didn't know who Rev was but they knew that the Zombies leader was insulated, protected by a trusted, apparently impenetrable core.

Rev was the brains and the decision-maker, but someone else—in truth, more than one someone else—handled day-to-day management. A brilliant decision on his part. He was protected and if even one the managers was arrested or God forbid, murdered, compromised in anyway, it wouldn't paralyze the Zombies.

As Musso and Maloney turned onto Valentine the scene brought to mind images on the evening news of streets in Somalia, the setting of the movie Blackhawk Down: on the sidewalk, an upturned car from the previous century, a pair of rubbish fires in rusted barrels, steel doors over once elegant entries and plywood in the windows of dilapidated, grief-stricken three-story brownstones. Most of the structures on Valentine—homes and businesses alike—were worn-out, eyesores, some with spray-painted gang markings, all in need of fresh paint, new wood, replacement siding or, to be torn down and rebuilt. Even in the unmarked Crown Vic, maybe *especially* in the unmarked Crown Vic,

Musso and Maloney were glared at by young kids with icy thousand-yard stares as they cruised the block. Might be dealers, might just be kids that didn't like cops. None of them did. They were taught at an early age to recognize and hate cops. The eyes and ears of the neighborhood. It looked like a slow day for the Zombies, though. At certain times there would be dozens of people milling about to buy crack and horse.

Maloney pulled the cruiser into a no-parking zone in front of a bodega, the center of commerce on this stretch of Valentine. Brightly colored neon signs advertising cervezas from south of the border, cigarettes, cheap pizza and lotto dominated the windows. A yellow and green neon sign read "Open". One might not know, otherwise. The store was dark in the gray of the overcast day. The owner was probably just trying to save money on electricity.

Exiting the radio patrol car, Musso encountered probably the last sound most people would expect in one of the world's largest cities: a gorilla rhythmically beating the tympani of his massive chest, carried on the wind, no more than a mile and a half as the crow flies from the Bronx Zoo, with over six hundred and fifty species and over six thousand animals, the largest in the country. Musso crouched, touched his service weapon, and scanned the landscape—the reaction natural after more than thirty years on the job, even if he would be surprised to see an ape swinging like Spider-Man along the building façades.

"Damn. I hate it when that happens," Musso said, a little embarrassed.

His partner, getting out of the squad car cautiously. "I know. You'd think we'd be used to it by now."

They entered the store to give the middle-aged latino proprietor some business and to try and earn some good will in return. The owner, with tattoo-covered arms showing below his short sleeves, black goatee turning to gray, propped on his elbows on the old, clouded, glass-topped candy-bar case—Three Musketeers, Snickers, Paydays and newer brands unrecognizable to anyone over twenty-five years old. Maloney picked out a pretty yellow banana from a wood bin of individual pieces of fruit, while Musso went to the bathroom.

As he ambled toward the rear of the store, glancing at the shelves, sparsely laden with goods, he asked, "Bathroom back here?"

"*Si*, meng, in the back ."

Musso followed the old worn, wide-plank wood floors to the rear of the store. They creaked from decades of use. The hand-lettered sign on the door read, *los baños*. Inside, the smell was bathroom cleaner overpowered by urine. The once-white porcelain toilet bowl, stained greenish-brown from the waterline down, hadn't been clean since World War II. After finishing he pulled the chain that hung from a tank mounted at the ceiling, to flush the ancient toilet. Washed up at the filthy sink, and, unwilling to touch the dirty faucet with his hands, turned off the water with his sleeve-covered elbow.

When he returned to the front he bought a taco with spicy ground beef and a Diet Pepsi.

Maloney had peeled the banana and was popping the last bite into his mouth.

"You know, if you're a real New Yorker you gotta drink Pepsi," Musso said as he tilted the light blue and red can in the direction of the Latino proprietor, "a New York company." He took a swallow and gazed at the rack of cigarettes behind the counter. Through his seasoned detective's eye he deduced that the tax stamps were counterfeit, but he wouldn't notify the feds—not yet anyway. The owner was just trying to help his bottom line a little. God knows running a business like this one, with out-of-control south Bronx rents, razor-thin margins and shoplifting punks eating up your profit had to be rough. But Carmine wouldn't hesitate to use the knowledge of the illegal stamps to his advantage if he needed to.

"So how's it going?" he asked the storeowner.

"Ah, you know, meng. This used to be a nice neighborhood. Nothing but losers now, drug dealers and whores. And I can't keep the *chavalos* from shoplifting. You know *chavalo*—punk?"

"*Si*, I know chavalo. Anyway, *mi amigo*, where are the dealers? Who's the worst? Where do we find him?"

"They all bad, meng." These cops with their practiced pleasantries made him nervous. "But I can't talk anymore. You need to leave. They see the *policia* in here they'll hurt my family."

Maloney couldn't deny they looked like cops. "Yeah, all right," he said, "but you call us if you think of anything we need to know," He handed the man his business card.

The proprietor didn't respond but merely gazed at the card with the imprint of a small gold-and-blue shield and NYPD in shiny dark-blue raised print. He couldn't read the detective's name—his English wasn't good enough—but he understood NYPD. He would get his son, a sophomore in high school, to read the name for him. Ironically, English was the son's best subject.

To try and reduce the risk to the storeowner they attempted to avoid the eyes of the neighborhood by slinking back to the car. Wished they could make themselves invisible. Try and undo any damage. The only person they passed on the sidewalk was a blind, octogenarian male Caucasian, his once cerulean blue eyes hidden by cataracts, with his worn-out old tan dog, sitting over a grate in the sidewalk, clouds of hot steam rising from it. He'd probably lived in the neighborhood most of his life. The man's green plaid flannel shirt, worn over a threadbare gray cardigan, in turn worn over a black hoodie, appeared warm but added nothing sartorially. A black stocking cap completed his outfit. Maloney felt sorry for him and hoped the man would use a donation to buy a scarf. He thought about buying one and bringing it back to him, but didn't know if the grate was his usual spot.

Maloney dropped a five-dollar bill in his cup, jostling it as he did to alert the man of the cash infusion. Some early Christmas goodwill. Trying not to stare, he noticed the old man hold the bill an inch from his eye in an attempt to make out the denomination.

"God Bless, you," the man said.

A middle-aged man standing at the corner loudly blew his nose into a handkerchief, a sound reminiscent of a honking goose.

"Well," Musso said, "that was a waste of time." Because Musso felt like his days on the job were coming to an end, he hated wasting time more than anything else and felt a visceral need to rid the streets of scum. He made a face and dropped the taco he'd just bought into a wire wastebasket. After the filthy restroom he couldn't bear the thought of a single bite

"Yeah, I just hope we didn't put that man and his family at risk."

"Yeah, me too. But I wish we had someone on the inside of the Zombies."

"Yeah, I know you do. You never give that a rest."

***

"Just a reminder, Rock—I have to get away on time this afternoon," said Maloney. "New quarter, you know." Maloney was going to law school at Columbia University at night and would be done in another year and a half. His father, John Sr., was a retired attorney and although senior was proud of him now, he'd been a little disappointed when John hadn't followed in his footsteps, doing it the way he did, attending law school right after undergrad. John had majored in Political Science at NYU and made the decision to follow his childhood dream and apply to the NYPD. Even when he was a kid, he'd admired the men in their sharply creased blue uniforms and loved watching homicide detectives ply their trade on television shows.

His father, on the other hand, right after completing his undergraduate degree at Harvard, matriculated at Harvard Law, and graduated number one in his class.

Eventually though, John, figuring better late than never—he was still young—pulled the metaphorical trigger and enrolled at Columbia Law, but his father, in his early seventies, was beginning to exhibit signs of early-onset dementia and John hoped his father would still know what was going on when he graduated, even though it wasn't that far off.

"I know. I haven't forgotten. No problem. We'll head back to the corral now and you can do what you gotta do."

"Thanks. We need to talk to that new snitch when we get back, anyways."

"Johnny, Johnny. We're supposed to call them confidential informants, CIs. Gotta be politically correct, you know. If I can learn to do it, you can too."

"I know, Carmine, I know. Wow. You're definitely an old dog and you're learning new tricks. I'm impressed."

"Smart ass."

***

Always one to give them some shit, Sergeant Cabrera said, "You yahoos back already?"

Musso said, "Yeah, slow day in the drug trade," Musso said. "They probably don't like the cold weather. But tomorrow's another day. Maybe you can go with us next time." Gave him some shit right back.

"Yeah, maybe I'll show youse guys how it's done."

In the break room, they talked to the new CI, Lamar, told him they needed anything he could get on the Zombies.

Musso: "You help us bring them down and you're gold. You'll get a commendation from the mayor himself."

"Well, just give me the gold. I can't eat a commendation. And remember the word on the street, if I need it, 'Warn a brother'." It was a reference to a T-shirt they'd seen with the movie studio's logo, with the play on words above it.

Maloney: "Come on, Lamar. You aren't supposed to be getting in trouble, now. You help the cops, you're supposed to be an upstanding citizen."

"I hear you, dude. But, just in case I have a relapse, forget I'm not supposed to break into apartments." Lamar wasn't really bad. He just smoked a little weed, sold a little on the side to finance his lifestyle, did a little B&E.

***

John Maloney was glad to to have a night at class. Mary Catherine had someone painting the apartment and he'd rather not have to smell the paint or put up with the mess any longer than he had to. Besides, he'd kind of gotten used to the beige walls. There was no need for designer colors all of a sudden.

After work and before he left for class, Maloney dropped by the Starshine Diner, one of his regular haunts, for dinner before driving into Manhattan to Columbia.

With its strong smell of grease and coffee, the diner had the ability to turn the stomach of someone with a weak constitution, but it was nearly full of people with strong stomachs or weak noses—men and women wearing the New York City uniform of dark colors, black or navy blue, jackets and outerwear, except for one elderly lady, already in the holiday spirit, wearing a well-worn, many-seasons-old Christmas sweater of green and red, that smelled of mothballs. In contrast to the other diners' dark shades her brightly-colored sweater and silver hair lightened up the room. The warm resonance of friendly conversations above the sound of flatware clattering was welcoming.

"What'll you have, baby?" the middle-aged server with copper-colored dyed hair said in her bourbon-laced smoker's voice from behind the stainless steel counter. She obviously wasn't eating the diner's food. She was five-foot-six and weighed no more than one hundred, one hundred-ten pounds. Johnny'd been seeing her at

Starshine for two-thirds of a decade and she still called him 'baby', never once asking his name. That's just the way New Yorkers were. She wore a light blue, mid-twentieth century waitress uniform. Her black nametag read BLANCHE.

He didn't bother looking at the menu she placed before him. It hadn't changed in six years and he always had the same meal. The silverware was placed neatly on a folded white cloth napkin.

"Meatloaf, mashed potatoes, green beans. Coffee, regular." In New York City vernacular regular meant with cream and sugar. Fewer words to say because everyone was in a hurry—even if they weren't.

Using a pencil retrieved from where it pierced the thick layers of her copper-colored hair, Blanche wrote the order down on an old school ticket pad.

"Be right out," she said as she clipped the light green-colored paper ticket on a clothespin hanging from a wire in the window open to the kitchen. "Order up," she shouted, so the cook could hear it above the din. Her voice larger than her small size. He shook his head slightly at her feeling she needed to yell.

She poured the coffee from a silver carafe into a heavy-sided white mug and set it down too hard, splashing some on the counter in front of him. "Oops," in place of an apology, and a tilt of her head in embarrassment, she found a dirty white hand towel and began to wipe up the spill. She hummed an unrecognizable tune while she cleaned the mess.

Johnny's cellphone, lying on the counter, rang, its vibration causing the surface to reverberate like a buzzing bee. New Jersey native Bruce Springsteen's *Born to Run* its ringtone. He saw Mary Catherine's initials, "MC", the nickname he used for his wife.

"Hey, babe…Yeah, left on time…I'm at Starshine…Getting a bite before class…I'll be home soon as it's over… About eleven…Love you too…I will…Bye."

The server topped off his coffee, altering the perfect blend of cream and sugar she'd concocted. Noticing a small jar with perforations in the lid and containing cinnamon sitting on the counter, he sifted some into his coffee, giving it a Christmasy taste. John hoped it wasn't an indication the diner was trying to turn into a yuppie establishment. He wasn't a fan of gentrification, hoping that the Bronx would never change. The restaurant held a dozen other patrons: working class, like him, mostly from South Bronx neighborhoods still living where they'd grown up, in the shadows of the George Washington Bridge, and in sight of the New Jersey Palisades. Although they didn't feel like they were trapped, most would never leave.

His food arrived. Meatloaf was a staple in New York City. A northern, cold weather comfort food. At Starshine you got three slices, tepee-ed over a pile of skin-on mashed potatoes. Good, hot food before going out into the chilly night.

Some restaurants tried to do too much to it: put a mixture of catsup with bell peppers on the meat and cook it with the topping. He preferred it cooked plain and adding his own catsup straight from the bottle on the counter. He pulled the pieces of meatloaf from the mound of potatoes, so he could drench them in tomatoey sauce. He was glad his brother-in-law wasn't there to witness it. The jerk had always said he used too much of it, like it was any of his business. After a dozen years of marriage Johnny still had to pretend to like him because he was Mary Catherine's brother, but they had nothing in common and both knew each didn't like the other. The brother liked to drink beer and smoke dope, and besides being a wine drinker, Johnny was a cop and had to look the other way when it came to the dope. They'd come to an agreement that he wouldn't smoke in front of Johnny and as long as he didn't, Johnny would forget that he knew about it. He cut off a piece with his fork then scooped up a bite of potatoes. The bite was still steaming and the food would warm him for the frosty night. The meatloaf was the perfect consistency—firm, but not cooked too hard, and the mashed potatoes had just a hint of lump in them reminding him that they were made from real potatoes and didn't come from a box.

"You Make it Feel Like Christmas" by Brooklynite, Neil Diamond, played over speakers hidden. It was the first Christmas song he'd heard this season. New York City loved its singers, no matter from which borough they came. Bing Cosby's "White Christmas" followed. Christmas music always put John in a festive mood, even though his job dealing with the city's worst criminal element didn't allow much time for celebrating. In years past he'd clad himself in padding and dressed in a rented, moth-worn Santa suit, delivered presents, which he and Mary Catherine had bought, by being frugal with their personal purchases, to a Bronx orphanage. As Johnny was finishing his supper Blanche offered a refill of coffee. Without looking at it, he covered the mug with his hand, his attention diverted by a noisy, apparently drunken man, who'd just entered the eatery. The man was loud, obnoxious, and starting to harass the diners, who just wanted to eat their suppers in peace and go home. Maloney could smell trouble along with the alcohol oozing from the drunk's pores.

"What a shitty place. Only old people and losers would eat in a joint like this. What are you looking at, lady? You're so old you probably can't even see me. Why'd I even come in this shitty place?" His machine-gun-fire monologue was directed at everyone and no one.

Turning to the one waitress working the tables, a cute brunette in her twenties, he said, "Hey, sweet cheeks, what're you doing later? Whatta ya say? Wanna go out, get a drink? I bet you're a white wine drinker. You look like you got class."

With a nervous look and a grimace on her face she did her best to ignore him and returned to clearing tables.

When the drunk put his hand on Maloney's shoulder, the detective slowly rotated on his barstool while retrieving the gold-and-blue shield of an NYPD detective from his jacket pocket. Unfolding it from its leather case and flipping it open in one deft move with his left hand was all he had to do to get the man to back off.

"Shorry, officer, no offense."

"Detective."

"Shorry?"

"It's not officer. It's Detective."

Shorry, Detective. I was just messin' around."

"It's called assault on a policeman. You're just lucky I've got somewhere I have to be. Don't have time to throw your sorry ass in jail."

Sobering quickly, eyes widening, he said, "Yes, sir. Thank you, sir."

Seeing that the man was contrite, or at least had the good sense to pretend to be, Maloney said, "You may go now."

He dipped a short, stiff bow and with his tail tucked between his legs left with none of the bravado with which he'd entered.

The cook-owner saw what Maloney had done and thanked him by tearing up the check for his meal.

"Thank you, Detective," he said.

"It was nothing. Just doing my job."

***

Johnny stepped outside. The streetlamps had come on while he was in the diner and shiny halos of spitting sleet and dancing snowflakes encircled the lights. A magical scene during the joyous Christmas season. He'd have to be watchful of icy patches on the drive to the Upper Westside. Stepping gingerly, he walked to his personal vehicle, a late-model, silver Honda Accord, crunching on the salt city workers had already begun spreading on the sidewalk. He'd parked in the next block and stepping off the sidewalk he splashed into a slushy puddle while making his way to the car. Gaining the Honda and stamping the icy water off his shoes, began to make his way to the Henry Hudson Parkway, where he pointed the small import south toward Manhattan. A few minutes later he passed the George Washington Bridge, connecting Manhattan to northern New Jersey, strung with lights to warn approaching vessels, on his right. Both upper and lower levels, referred to by locals as George and Martha, which he'd always thought clever, were gridlocked both east and west with after-work traffic. It wasn't long before he got off at 96th Street and turned left then left again to head back north on Broadway to the Columbia University campus. The wide boulevard had earned its broad name and was shiny with rain and ice, the red-and-green traffic lights' reflections, appropriate for the approaching holiday season, glistening in the wet roadway. He passed Tom's Diner, the stand-in for Monk's on television's Seinfeld, at the corner of 112th Street. Seeing it always gave him a contented feeling. Out-of-town friends usually asked him to take them there for its inexpensive, tasty food and atmosphere reminding them of the iconic sitcom about nothing.

As the outline of the school's buildings appeared ahead of him he was reminded of why he loved the Columbia University campus, voted by a leading architectural publication as one of the ten most beautiful in the country. With his near eidetic memory He recalled the literature given him when he'd matriculated describing how it began in 1754 as Kings College, and was later redesigned in the Beaux Arts Style by McKim, Mead and White, the architecture firm that designed Penn Station, the original New York Life building, the Washington Square Arch and the second Madison Square Garden. Johnny prided himself in being an amateur New York City historian and could recite the city's history chapter-and-verse back to Pre-Revolutionary war.

Chapter Three
SWAT

The icy weather slowing him down, Maloney didn't get home from class until almost eleven-thirty the previous night. Even so, he decided to get in a workout before his shift. At six a.m. it was still dark outside. He brushed light sleet from the shoulders of his overcoat as he hurried into the building to gain shelter from the coldest hour of the day, Having a well-equipped weight room in the precinct meant he had no excuse for not lifting, so most weeks he got in at least three workouts. He started with bench press, and unlike most people, after a warm-up set he'd start with heavier weights and then go lighter, his unassailable logic being he was able to keep his reps higher on each set. Today he did a set of ten with two hundred twenty-five pounds, and after a ninety-second rest dropped the weight to one-eighty-five and got another ten before finishing with one-fifty-five for twelve reps. At a height of five-foot ten and the same buck seventy-five he'd maintained since his college days, he felt good about the weight and the reps. He wasn't as lean as he'd been in college, but he wasn't exactly in the average category yet, either. Somewhere between athletic and average, which was fine at thirty-five.

After shoulder presses, he worked on inclined dumbbell presses and then did some ab work, before going down the hall to a small room where a masseuse was set up and waiting. The Chinese masseuse bowed to him as he entered and gestured toward her sheet-covered massage table. Hopping up on it and laying face down, he told her he wanted a hard Thai-style massage. The weekly free massages were a great job perk. The woman was much stronger than she appeared and after the better part of an hour, he left the room hurting and with legs so weak it would take him a couple of cups of caffeine before he'd have the energy to walk normal.

After showering he was at his desk working on his first cup when Musso came in. He eschewed the breakroom paper cups for his large mug with the Batman wing logo decorating it. He justified a kid's curiosity by saying the Batman was a crime fighter and so was he. He'd bought it in a souvenir shop at the South Street Seaport downtown after he and MC had had lunch at Fraunces Tavern, which had served as

George Washington's headquarters and where the general gave a farewell address to his officers. The amateur historian in him loved visiting New York's historic sites.

The coffee sucked but it was caffeine and it was hot and free. Besides, he wasn't about to spend four-fifty for a latte at Starbucks. He thought those who did were wasting their money, agreeing with George Carlin when the comedian said, *if you order a triple, mocha, venti, choco, latte, whatever, you're just an asshole.*

"Mornin,' partner." Musso looked tired and even more rumpled than usual.

"How ya doin?"

"Ahh, I'll be okay after some caffeine."

"Well, what're you waiting for? Let's get you some."

In the break room, Detective Musso poured six ounces into a generic white cup, ashamed of itself for not wearing a green logo. Added some French Vanilla powdered creamer someone had donated, and two packages of sugar to the concoction to try and render it drinkable. He took a gulp and made a face. It hadn't worked. "Ow!" No insulated sleeve caused it to scorch the tips of his fingers. Double the indignity.

Recovering from scorched fingers and the bitter taste in his mouth, Musso asked "You get a workout this morning?" Detecting, he'd noticed a slight sheen on Maloney's forehead and deduced the film was from a hot shower.

"Yeah, chest and shoulders."

"Good, if something falls on me, you can lift it off."

"You can count on me, Rock." Musso's irony was in full force. Years spent boxing had left him a powerfully built, barrel-chested man; the last thing he needed was help with heavy lifting.

Musso wandered to the east-facing window, where he gazed at the buildings of Coop City in the distance, Thankful they'ed been successful in that large complex so far, giving the solidly middle-income families a safe place to live.

The lieutenant rushed in. "You guys're up, right?" He knew they were, knew the schedule better than the detectives did. "We got a big one. A uni saw some bad guys trying to hijack an armored truck in front of the Wells Fargo branch on East 149th. Called it in. He's on the scene. Go get 'em. Let's roll," His dramatic baritone, honed from years performing with the Lincoln Center Theatre, went up an octave when he was distressed, like now.

"Got it, Lou," said Musso. He made a face as the bad coffee, growing tepid, changed to worse. He was happy to toss it. Maloney poured his in the sink and ran some water in the big mug that everybody knew was his.

***

En route to the Wells Fargo branch they were patched through to the uniform officer on site, who sounded rattled.

"They shot the two guards and got in the armored truck. Detectives, they have some serious firepower. Damned assault rifles. I've got their truck blocked with my cruiser."

Maloney took a deep breath, then said, "Ahh…that might not have been the best move…"

Before Maloney could finish his thought, the cop on scene shouted, "Wait, they're starting the truck." Maloney heard the sound of metal crunching and felt as much as heard the movement of the radio patrol car over the radio. "Hold it…Oh Jesus, they just smashed into the cruiser, pushed it out of the way."

Musso: "Don't do anything. It's okay. Armored trucks have GPS tracking on them. We'll be able to follow it. Just back off, don't put yourself in danger. Roger that?"

The cop did so, then Musso radioed the lieutenant. "Talked to the uniform. Both guards are down and the perps have flown in the truck. Can you talk to the armored company, get them to track it?"

"Will do, Musso. Back in a couple." Thinking they were too cool for it, Bronx detectives dispensed with the usual police formalities on the radio.

"Okay, we're rolling an ambulance. Dispatch is going to put the armored company through to you and they'll put you on the BG's trail. We're sending the ESU, but you guys are point until they get there."

"Standing by," Musso responded calmly.

The Emergency Service Unit (ESU) was a subset of the Special Operations Division, NYPD's version of a SWAT—always on patrol, all three tours, 365 days a year, including Christmas, with ten Heavy Rescue trucks to assist in dicey situations.

"Excuse me, Detectives?" The armored company's dispatcher didn't talk to law enforcement very often and was suffering from a mild case of the nerves. He sounded young.

"Yeah, we're here."

"Ah, they're…they're heading west on surface streets."

Musso: "You can bet your ass they're gonna get on 87, going north." Interstate 87, also known as the New York State Thruway, went upstate to rural New York.

Maloney nodded. "Yeah, but they're probably just winging it. Flying by the seat of their pants. I guarantee you this wasn't part of their plan." They were talking to themselves as if the person on the radio weren't there.

"Detectives?"

Maloney: "Yeah?"

"Uh, they're getting on 87-North at Gun Hill Road,"

Maloney: "Bingo—Gun Hill's sure as hell gonna slow 'em down,"

Musso: "Us, too. Sheesh, Gun Hill on a Tuesday morning."

Musso lived near Gun Hill and knew how bad the traffic on the major artery could be.

Gridlocked traffic and thousands of shoppers, businessmen and - women plus tourists clogging the thoroughfare and sidewalks—no way they'd be able to get through fast enough, Needing a different route to the thruway, they took 149th East to The Grand Concourse, then followed it north, until it intersected with the Cross Bronx Expressway, I-95, then again east on 95 until it connected with I-87.

Once on 87, Maloney and Musso opened up the Crown Vic Police Interceptor's large V-8, closing the distance between them and the heavy armored truck. They were the only team that had not yet moved to the smaller Ford Taurus. Musso liked the generous cabin and the bigger V-8. What he'd told the bosses was *over my fucking dead body.* Age and seniority sometimes carried with them perks.

Musso: "We just got on 87 at 95,"

"The truck just passed 225th Street. You're about two miles behind."

"Thanks for the update. Keep us posted."

"Will do, detectives." The dispatcher was loosening up. The game was definitely afoot.

Maloney sped up, setting the cruise control on eighty. No need to be crazy about it. With the company tracking the armored truck's GPS, the perps wouldn't get away.

Ten minutes later: "No change, still going north on 87."

"Roger that. Why don't you update us every five?"

"Will do detective."

On the radio, the lieutenant: "ESU is rolling and they have a chopper about to lift off."

"Thanks, Lou."

Maloney: "A chopper'll work. They sure as hell won't get away now."

One of the heavy-duty ESU trucks would level the playing field if they tried ramming or pushing anymore radio patrol cars out of the way. And the helicopter would assure they would ensure visual contact.

A few minutes later: "Detectives?"

"Yes."

"They're leaving the freeway at Exit 21. Going west."

"Thanks."

"That's one exit north of Woodstock," Musso said. "Nothing but cows and pine trees up there."

Maloney, not to be outdone, replied, "And with all the artsy-fartsy types in Woodstock nearby, as Lou Gossett said in *An Officer And A Gentleman*, 'Nothing but steers and queers.' "

"Hey, I'm the one that's supposed to say inappropriate things like that, not you."

"You must be rubbin' off on me, partner. Anyway only about ten more miles. I better step on it."

Leaning over to look skyward through the windshield, Musso said, "Look, there's the chopper."

"Good, they can run but they can't hide."

Before reaching their exit, they passed the one for Bethel, NY, famous for Max Yasgur's six-hundred acre farm where the Woodstock Festival was held and attended by four hundred thousand people in August of 1969. Another time it would have caused the friends to argue about music; old school rock versus new and various artists. But this was not a time for levity. The men they were chasing had already killed two bank guards and the detectives needed to stay focused on the deadly task at hand.

"Detectives, they've stopped."

"Okay, you talking to the ESU chopper?"

"Affirmative."

"Can you patch us through to them?"

"Will do. Stand by."

The dispatcher said, "Gentlemen, you don't need us anymore. Good luck."

"Roger that. Detectives Maloney and Musso here."

"Sergeant Woska, speaking."

"Sergeant, you have their position?"

"Affirmative. About a mile and a half off the exit, west of the freeway, on the right. Looks like an abandoned convenience store. Turn right next to it. A quarter mile down that road, turn left on a gravel road, a country lane. Another quarter mile and it dead-ends at an abandoned two-story house. The truck is parked behind it."

"Thanks. We'll be there ASAP. Probably less than fifteen."

"Ten-Four. Don't engage until the cavalry gets there. The heavy artillery is about fifteen behind you."

"Ten-Four." Maloney thought since the sergeant was playing the formal radio game, he'd would, too. To his partner, Musso said, "They must be familiar with the area."

Left the freeway at Exit 21 to turn west toward Catskill. A train of at least two dozen motorcycles passed them as they slowed to get on the country route. Their license tags were from Virginia. On a road trip. DOT Orange barrels shut down half of the exit lane. Turning left on the rural two-lane roadway, the last remnants of autumn leaves waltzed on the highway less-traveled. It appeared that the only thing holding up a dilapidated white clapboard church was a no trespassing sign affixed to the double front doors. Passed a cemetery with graves from two centuries before, it giving away to open land littered with mobile homes common to this part of rural upstate New York.

"Did you see that?" Musso said.

"No. I'm driving. See what?"

"That shack back there—in upstate New York, no less—had a rebel flag hanging on the front porch." A worn out old house, in need of paint and new wood siding, probably built in the twenties.

"Get outta here."

"I shit you, not."

"Probably a transplanted southern extremist."

"I'd bet twenty bucks he's on a terrorist watch list."

"I'm not gonna take that bet."

A highway sign on the weak shoulder, partially obscured by high weeds, read WOODSTOCK 4 MILES. Approaching the ancient convenience store/service station the sergeant described, they pulled into the parking lot of a boarded-up Hess Oil station and food mart. Overgrown grass pierced the broken concrete.

Musso said, "Boy this place brings back memories."

"Of what?"

"You're too young to remember. But, back when I was a young punk, Hess Oil stations were like the North Pole for kids. Rows and rows of stuffed animals of all types and colors stacked to the ceilings. It was paradise."

"You're right I am too young to remember that."

Musso shrugged as if to say, "Your loss." Then, "Okay. Get your game face on. Focus."

As the vehicle skidded to a stop, Maloney popped the trunk for them to armor up. After climbing into their vests, they each retrieved Mossberg 590A 12-gauge shotguns. In the fresh morning air the fragrant scent of surrounding pines enveloped them like the vests they climbed into.

Getting back in their vehicle, they made their way down the side road next to the station and, as the crumbling macadam ended, reached the unpaved gravel road on the left. They rolled down the windows hoping they wouldn't hear the sounds of gunfire that would be warning of an ambush. The only noise, the sound of tires crunching on gravel.

Maloney pulled over on the right side of what had narrowed to a two-track, keeping a copse of trees between them and a once elegant summer home belonging to someone from the Big Apple. The front entry was a half-moon terrace with four fluted columns rising to support the portico two stories above. The right-side entrance was covered by a porte cochere, beneath which revelers once exited their cars to attend Gatsby-worthy parties and teas.

On three sides of the now disheveled home, dense old-growth hardwoods interspersed among evergreens of various varieties, blocked the direct morning sunlight, making the moldy forest floor spookily full dark.

Exiting the cruiser, Musso and Maloney heard only wind echoing through the pines and the *hooing* of an owl on the elm tree branch above them, denuded earlier than normal due to the unusual—even for upstate New York—early season cold. Bouquets of mistletoe decorated occasional naked tree limbs. As Musso climbed out he stretched a broad stride attempting, without success to span an icy, mud-colored puddle. "Good job of parking, partner. Thanks for putting me in the crap. Damn, and a new pair of shoes, too." He'd had them for over a year—but that *was* new to Musso. He was known around the precinct for being cheap. *He* called it being frugal.

After a couple of minutes, the roar of a large diesel engine coming from a troop carrier emblazoned with the emblem of the NYPD ESU arrived moments before the vehicle emerged from behind the trees. It drowned out the white noise of the traffic on the New Jersey turnpike and frightened a school of blackbirds into flight. Pulling to a stop, eight officers in black riot gear with full body armor, helmets with dark shaded face shields and wielding Colt M4A1 AR15-type automatic rifles, spilled out, looking either comforting or discomforting, depending on one's point of view.

The icy wind in the old trees grew bolder as if angry at the loud diesel for trying to drown it out.

One of the helmeted, armored, storm troopers approached Musso and Maloney.

"Commander Kevin O'Hearn," he said while snapping off a crisp salute. He held a mug of coffee in his free hand. *They must have their own stash in the carrier.* Musso wondered if it was any better than the offering at the precinct. Probably way better—the ESU was the department's golden boys and got nothing but the best.

"Coffee?" One of the troopers offered them a cup.

"Musso said, "Don't mind if I do."

Maloney said, "Thought you'd never ask."

The coffee *was* better than the swill at Fort Apache and it provided warmth against the early morning bitter cold of the upstate New York countryside. Musso would have to remember to talk to the lieutenant.

"Whatta we got?" Unable to see the team leader's face through the blacked-out faceshield was a little off-putting, bringing to mind dark images of Darth Vader. Finally raising it to down some coffee, he was a large, solidly built man with a rugged jawline—and looked like he could play linebacker for the hometown Giants.

"We just got here," said Musso, "and the lieutenant said you were in charge. Just tell us what you want us to do."

Commander O'Hearn was confident if nothing else. "I'll talk to them. Take their temperature. Boatman, get me the megaphone." He made the command sound like the most important decision ever made.

"Yes, sir." A short, skinny, hirsute officer retrieved the megaphone from the vehicle.

From the cover provided by the ESU truck, O'Hearn spoke into the handheld. "Attention in the house."

The response was immediate—automatic gunfire in the form of the bad guys' own AR-15s. From two locations in the old mansion a total of about sixty rounds ricocheted off the heavily armored truck. They obviously were prepared with multiple thirty-round magazines. Although the .223 caliber rounds tearing into flesh and bones, would mess up a person's day, they did nothing more than scratch the paint of the personnel carrier's armor.

O'Hearn said, "Damn, if I bring back another shot-up truck the captain's going to have my ass." Then he shrugged and downed another gulp of coffee, swishing it around in his mouth before he swallowed, then said, "fuck it." Even one of the largest police departments in the world had to be cognizant of its budget. "I keep telling him it's just one of the hazards of the job."

On first impression Maloney and Musso liked O'Hearn, A professional who possessed a healthy *I don't-give-a-shit* attitude." That would take him far in the department.

"Okay, these guys want to play hardball, we have the toys for it." He spoke into a small mic attached to his collar, "Fire her up."

The back door of the armored carrier opened and a small four-wheeled vehicle the size of a golf cart, with puffs of smoke, belched to life and rolled to the ground on aluminum tracks. Far more intimidating in appearance than a golf cart, however, its armor-covered body bore the ESU shield; the only opening a small port the size of a mail slot, it covered by bullet-proof glass, through which the driver could see to navigate. Carrying four team members, the vehicle was able to cross the open ground to the once stately mansion without exposing the squad to enemy fire.

High above, the ESU helicopter hovered at five hundred feet to provide cover if needed, with its war-tested fifty-caliber machine gun.

The home's main entry, about fifty yards away, was the goal of the tiny squad. The small tank-like vehicle had steel wheels with tracks instead of rubber tires as to cause it to be unaffected by gunshots trying to stop it. The steel tracks caused the small tank to be slow moving, however, and it took them about three minutes to cross the open ground. Drawing fire from the two upstairs windows as it advanced was disconcerting to the team, due to the sound of the bullets hitting the vehicle, but had no more effect than being a noisy nuisance in the small steel chamber as scores of rounds reverberated off it.

Once the four-man ESU squad reached the house, the three with assault rifles flanked the doorway and one officer, the largest one with the most muscle, bearing a forty pound hand-held battering ram, positioned himself two feet from the door, planted his feet in a karate-style front stance, and swinging the ram just below waist high and aiming inside the lock of one of the solid wood doors, with one blow shattered it, leaving it hanging from its hinges.

O'Hearn hated the term "assault" weapon, knowing it was a pejorative created by politicians to stir up emotions in the citizenry. He preferred the term "tactical weapon", but simply stated; they were rifles, but that didn't sound nearly as terrifying as "assault" weapons.

The door-blaster pivoted ninety degrees to the right in an attempt to make himself skinny to avoid the other three team members. And his fellow officers exploded past him, entering high and low. They had rehearsed the entry ad nauseam until each knew where the others would be, like football players on a well-tuned offense. It was most likely that the shooters were still upstairs, but more serious than a football game, being cautious was the way the team returned to play again.

Through the Bluetooth earbud he wore, the team lead, First Officer Jim Frost, heard Commander O'Hearn:

"We still see the perps upstairs. We'll keep them busy. Be alert and get home safe." He ordered the remainder of the team to pour continuous automatic fire on the two windows to let the perps know they had to pay attention to them. And along with Musso and Maloney they opened fire. Soon, the 223 caliber rounds and 12-gauge shotgun pellets hammered the stucco exterior walls surrounding the windows, giving them an acne-scarred appearance.

Using hand signals to communicate, Officer Frost told one team member to stay downstairs to cover their six, while he took point.

Leading his team, they ascended the once magnificent broad staircase with trepidation, knowing they were easy targets for anyone waiting at the top. They moved with stealth and speed to reduce their time in the danger zone.

Fortunately for them the bad guys were busy keeping their heads down from the fire outside. They were not met by gunfire from the second floor. Frost dropped behind a waist-high stone vase, a second officer ducked into the threshold of an open bedroom, each of them covering opposite ends of the hallway as the third dropped to the floor and, lying on his back, as if pierced by a spindle, pivoted his weapon in each direction, providing cover on both ends of the hallway if needed.

Although confident they knew which rooms the gunmen were in, working under standard operating procedure they checked each of the doors they encountered.

Leaving one officer at the top of the staircase to cover their rear, the other two moved toward the north end of the structure. The sound of shooting continued both from their team outside and the last room on the right.

They quickly checked three rooms just to be sure they wouldn't be surprised by other gunmen. Upon reaching the room from which the shooting was heard, Officer Frost pulled the pin from a stun grenade and, opening the door a crack, squatted and rolled it into the room.

The flash made sight impossible for about five seconds and the loud blast would cause a temporary loss of hearing, vertigo and loss of balance. Those actions gave them their nicknames: flash-bang grenades.

The subsequent blast was unbearable and the flash blinding; but not to the ESU team who, knowing what to expect and being prepared, wore earplugs and shut their eyes. Immediately after the concussion they rushed the disoriented gunman, who, blood pouring from his ears, was subdued, checked for other weapons, and cuffed. Then, knowing the hallway was clear, they sprinted to the room on the other end, but as Frost tossed a second stun grenade into the room he was hit by a bullet in the chest. The impact—like that of a sledgehammer—knocked him off his feet, but the grenade still did its job and after pulling the man's hands from his bleeding ears and pinning them behind his back, the second officer body-pinned the stunned and dazed suspect to the ground and cuffed him. Fortunately for Frost, his body armor did its job as well as the stun grenade did its. He would have a painful bruise on his chest for a couple of weeks but he would be no worse for the wear.

Frost spoke into his mic: "Sergeant, threats are neutralized. Send two men to assist in moving suspects." Since he was injured, Frost didn't want to take any chances with them.

"Roger that."

The two officers arrived and with the assistance of the third they'd left at the staircase, the suspects were escorted to their ESU truck, where they were caged for transport.

Commander O'Hearn said self-satisfied and smugly, "We're heading to the barn."

Musso, attempting to sound just as smug, said, "Our barn, right?"

***

Back at Fort Apache Lieutenant Michael Shapiro saw his returning detectives and said, "I need a debrief, stat."

Maloney said, "No problem, Lou. Give us five."

Later, after giving the lieutenant the rundown, Shapiro said, "Good job. I knew you'd take care of it."

"Lou, it wasn't us. Those ESU guys are the best,"Maloney said. "They perform like an elite military unit and they run their plays as good as the Jets. And I know Carmine won't mind me speaking for him. We'd work with those guys again any time."

Musso grunted his agreement. "Except they're more like the Giants instead of those fucking Jets.

"Now, now, Musso. Play nice. But good to know. Anyway, good work. Now get back to the regular job."

"Will do, Lou."

Chapter Four
The Zombies

'Rev had a bad feeling. He believed in the tenets of Sun Tzu's *Art of War* and he was at the second of the three levels of war: he knew himself but he didn't know his enemy, law enforcement. More precisely, he didn't know what they knew about him or his operation. That was better than the lowest level: you don't know your enemy or yourself. But he hadn't attained the highest level of fulfillment yet, where you know yourself and know your enemy.

He had survived as the most successful drug dealer in the Bronx by being knowledgable. Knowledge was power. Knowing what the police were doing, what the competition was up to and what his people were doing.

An exciting idea, so clever it even surprised him, came to mind. Find someone, a street person as he had once been, place him on the inside and feed the pigs minor information about the Zombies. But the plant's real purpose would be to get Rev info on the cops, what they knew about Rev and what they had planned for him.

Rev called together his inner circle, the four men he knew he could trust with his life, and his fortune. He knew it because he had already, many times before.

He'd grown up with Marquise. They'd met on the playground of PS 46, Edgar Allan Poe Elementary School, in first grade, and had been friends ever since. Another kid, smaller but more aggressive than the already-big-for-his-age Marquise, was picking on him. Rev, then known only as James, came to his rescue, went upside the other kid's head, and Marquise pledged undying fealty to James, his devotion shown many times over. What he'd said was, "You can count on me, little bro. Forever." Twenty-five years later, it was still true.

Although Marquise was a gentle giant, his presence and stature were frightening. Topping six-foot-seven and weighing in at over three hundred pounds, his shiny head was the size of a basketball, his hands literally the size of catchers' mitts, his baggy-style jeans were tight on his massive thighs. Had he cared more about his studies Marquise would have continued playing the o-line after high school, but graduation had marked the end of his glory days.

Marquise was head of operations for the Zombies. He recruited new dealers and helped them build their support network. And they were all afraid of him. No dealer would dream of ripping off the Zombies or going out on their own.

Darelle was a natural math genius. He kept the Zombie's books, the Profits & Losses and kept track of their legal investments. His ledger was never far from his side. He could talk street as well as any corner dealer but could speak the King's English with attorneys and corporate bankers. He'd been Rev's quarterback on the high school football team and they'd developed a rapport typical of that between quarterback and wideout that would serve them well in their role as leaders of the Zombies, even with their roles reversed, since Rev was definitely the signal caller of the group. Darelle had a shiny black, perfectly round head and wore round-framed, non-prescription wire-rimmed spectacles, because he thought they enhanced his financial expert image and gave him a respectful look. That was in contrast to the diamond studs as big as thumbnails he wore in his pierced ears to give an edgy air to his well-crafted appearance. The organization's trio of accountants reported to him.

Lawrence Thompson, LT, was a Harvard Law School-educated attorney, older than the others except for Incognito; in his mid-40s, he moved with the grace and poise of a former athlete. Except when in a meeting, or court, he preferred track suits and athletic shoes, and gold chains adorning his neck. He and Rev had met at his father's church: LT being one of the ones that Rev was jealous of, for his father having a good relationship with, although the two of them had been able to work it out. Although he'd had a thriving practice, he'd quickly figured out that he could make a better living working for only one client— Rev.

Carmelito Incognito, who always introduced himself as Harry— was the only non-African-American in upper management with the Zombies. He took the name Harry as his own from the huge Harry Winston diamonds he wore. A matching pinkie ring, tie tack and cufflinks. Rev and Carmelito met, when Rev, even though he was hesitant to go because he didn't finish his degree requirements, attended a Colombia alumni event and although Incognito had been at the school fifteen years previous, they immediately liked each other, bonded, exchanged numbers, then met for dinner and thought it made sense for the Italiano to go to work for Rev. In charge of security, he was also Rev's unofficial bodyguard. He looked like a cross between the now middle-aged former *Friends* star Matthew Perry and a younger Al Pacino. Harry's fingers resembled Italian sausages. Harry Winston-designed platinum-set four-carat diamond cluster adorned his left pinkie, although to call the Italian sausage-like appendage a pinkie was comical. While others dressed casually, Harry wore black—suit, shirt and tie, for which he was known. The diamond tie-tack that held the cravat immobile matched the pinkie ring, and his cufflinks completed the set. His shiny black hair, was dyed, styled and sprayed straight back from his forehead. First-generation Italian, he told people his ancestors were Sicilian, due to its perceived connection to *La Familia,* and he always referred to the Zombies as "Our Thing," the literal translation of la Cosa Nostra. No one knew if Harry was truly Sicilian or not, but no one dared question it—at least, not to his face.

To the table Rev spoke: "Good evening, Gentlemen." They met in the dining room of the old brownstone owned by a Zombies corporation. Darelle believed in diversification and intended to protect James's assets through wise investments. They sat around an old but elegant dining table that could have seated ten. Their meetings always held an element of tension because, even though most of them had been friends for years, their business relationship was deadly serious, born of running a highly illegal eight figure enterprise with the ever present threat of prison or death. None of them wanted to incur Rev's wrath.

A knock at the door and a young man entered carrying two bottles of chilled Moscato and five wine glasses on a Wilton polished-pewter tray. He was a low-level runner of the sort they brought in to serve them whenever they had their periodic meetings. A different one each time, Rev didn't know their names and didn't want to know them. They would then be sent to the North Bronx with no chance of more contact with them. If Rev felt particularly paranoid the server would be disappeared, although he tried not to do that. Rev poured a glass of the ubiquitous, sweet, pink-hued wine popularized by hip-hop artists and rappers, drew in a mouthful, smiled and gestured for the server to pass the bottles and glasses around the table.

Although Rev didn't complete his degree requirements at Columbia, he'd continued to educate himself, to polish himself in much the same way craftsman had polished the pewter serving tray. He was knowledgeable about philosophy, Broadway theatre, world history and wine, and had an extensive vocabulary. He liked having a home filled with fine furnishings. He was proud of his knowledge and lifestyle and didn't mind showing it off when the opportunity arose.

Pleased with himself and his nascent plan, Rev smiled broadly and opened his arms wide. "I have an idea I want to run by you, my brothers. I think we need someone on the inside with the police to report to us, keep us abreast of their movement, of what they know about us. I was thinking we'd get one of our dealers arrested, set him up as one of their CI's. But instead of him giving them info, he'd feed us what they know." He smiled again and glancing from each to the next, studied their eyes, knowing them well enough to know that they were accepting it already. "What do you think?"

"Wouldn't the pigs expect info from him?" The question was from Marquise.

"He would give them small bits and pieces. Info that wouldn't hurt us. As long as he gave them something it would keep them hooked and wanting more."

"Assuming we do it, how do we choose our man?" from Harry.

"That will be Marquise's job. He knows his people. He will select three or four that he feels good about. You, Carmelito, will vet them." Rev was the only one who could get away with calling him Carmelito. No one else would dare to call him anything but his preferred Harry. "You all will interview each of them. Pick the one you think is best and I'll make the final decision. Of course in circumstances like these he won't know who any of us are."

Darrelle spoke up. "We can always use information. Information is money in all businesses. Our's is no different than any other in that respect."

LT nodded his acceptance.

They all agreed.

"It's settled then," Rev said. "Get started please, Marquise."

"I'm on it, boss," the big man responded.

***

"I'm going to the Pound. You want to join me for a pint?" Musso asked Maloney referring to the neighborhood watering hole most of the detectives hung out at after hours, as he turned off his computer.

"I can have a couple before I go home."

"I didn't say anything about a couple." He didn't miss the chance to bust his partner's balls whenever he got the chance. "You're always pushing the envelope. You ready?"

"You go on. Give me five."

"Sounds good."

Literally around the corner from Fort Apache, the Dog Pound, the quintessential New York policeman's bar and neighborhood dive. A green artificial Christmas tree strung with old-style, multi-colored lights divided the area between the bar and the dining area. Another festive tree hung upside down from the ceiling. NY Giants and Yankees memorabilia decorated the walls. The highlight; a Giants helmet hand-painted and embellished on every inch, by the world famous pop artist, Peter Max. The bar owner had won it by being the highest bidder on an eBay auction. It had cost him over three thousand dollars before the others dropped out. He thought it gave the bar some class. The tables and booths had small shaded lamps, providing little light, helpful for ambiance but not in illuminating the stains. The bar needed the help with ambiance. Fifties era, traditional Christmas carols blared from the eight-track player in the four-decades-old sound system. The owner would have liked to have gotten some newer Christmas music but nothing new was available on eight-track tapes. Bing Crosby's "White Christmas" set the mood for the start of the holiday season.

Musso was leaning against the over fifty year old scarred mahogany bar and was three-quarters of the way through his pint of Gun Hill Gold, a local Bronx microbrew, when Maloney arrived. His elbows fitted perfectly into light spots rubbed into the dark wood by a half-century of customers standing at that very spot, looking much like one of the Earp brothers standing at the bar in the Crystal Palace Saloon in Tombstone.

Maloney ordered his usual. "Brendan, gimme a Guinness, with a big head?" He raised the inflection at the end as if it were a question, and like Brendan would say "no" if he didn't. Of course he might have refused to pour it with the big head. Brendan couldn't understand why anyone would drink a beer like that. Although Maloney preferred wine—especially with good food—in a police hangout he always drank beer.

"You got it, Johnny." In a real cool practiced bartender's move, Brendan popped the top off the bottle of Guinness letting it fly through the air to land on the floor in front of the bar. He'd have to remember to pick it up before someone slipped on it and fell.

Brendan was in his early forties, dressed in a white dress shirt with a clip-on black bow-tie underneath a long burgundy canvas apron. His father had opened the iconic South Bronx bar before he was born. And under the son's watch it was more popular than ever. Especially with the detectives from Fort Apache and a few of the neighborhood regulars. He brought in musicians a few times, a couple of acoustic guitarists, a keyboardist—a young Asian man, a senior music major at NYU, a terrific song writer—hoping live music might bring in more business, but most of the cops just thought it was annoying and interfered with talking about the job and arguing about the Giants vs. the Jets. And the ones that did like the music were mostly of an age that couldn't agree on what except that it should be old school rock and roll, so he didn't make music permanent.

Glancing around the Pound Maloney grew thoughtful. "You know Rock, I like this place better at Christmas than any other time of year. The tree and decorations and seeing the snow through the windows really bring out it's old world charm. What do you think?"

"What do I think? I think you ought to be a goddamn poet, John. You're too damn sensitive to be a cop."

"Real funny, Rock."

A woman they didn't recognize, standing near them, resembled a young Carole King, ordered a *slightly* dirty martini, with blue cheese olives. Musso thought sheesh, a *slightly* dirty martini? She must be a challenge. Although attractive, he was glad she wasn't his wife. She looked at the two detectives sheepishly and said, "Some bartenders put far too much olive juice in their martinis, so slightly dirty is better, and, you simply must have it with blue cheese olives. Don't you agree?"

Musso turned his back, already growing tired of her. Maloney tilted his mug to her in a gesture he hoped looked like agreement, but wouldn't encourage conversation since, explaining her drink choice, he thought she sounded a bit defensive.

She took a swallow and said, "Shit, too much damn olive juice."

She sent it back and said, "Just give me a Stoli's Oliver's Twist." Said with attitude, she obviously hadn't learned the old saw that your neighborhood bartender can be your best friend. Although he didn't get many requests for it in a tough south Bronx neighborhood cop bar, Brendan knew that it was one of the newer yuppie drinks, vodka on the rocks with a lemon twist and an olive. But he wasn't impressed with her choice of vodka.

She looked at Maloney, shook her head, and said, "Maybe he can get that right."

Brendan asked, "Have you ever tried Tito's vodka?"

"I like Stoli's" was her exasperated reply.

"Okay, I was just trying to help."

"The best way you can help is by making me a Stoli's Oliver's Twist," was her rude reply.

Maloney drank his beer old school, picking up a saltshaker and sprinkling some of the white stuff into the heavy glass mug, in an attempt to make the head even thicker. He licked at the resultant thick layer of foam since his favorite uncle, the black sheep of the family, had taught him to drink it that way. His father had never forgiven his older brother for that one and Johnny couldn't help but think fondly of his late Uncle Padraig when he tasted a Guinness.

"Youse need another one?" Brendan asked.

Glancing at his watch, Maloney said, "I can have one more before the wife gets too pissed off."

Having just tossed a handful of bar nuts into his mouth, Musso tapped the lip of his mug with two fingers, indicating his desire for another.

Brendan asked John. "Do you want a new mug or does that one have sentimental value?"

"Smart ass."

"Hey, you shouldn't call your bartender names."

" My bartender shouldn't be a smartass."

A man down the bar, from the neighborhood, said to his friend, "I play poker with a couple of crazy Pakistanis." He kept his chin tucked into the collar of his dress shirt in an effort to hide his crow's neck.

***

The morning dawned shiny and bright, the previous day's snow and sleet moving east to drench the Atlantic. The brilliant sun did nothing to warm the temperature, however; it still hovered in the upper twenties. Shadows of tree branches splintered the sidewalk on which Maloney advanced toward Fort Apache, with the sailing silhouettes of two pigeons far above flashing their umbras. Even though it was frigid, the welcome sunshine fueled the spring in Maloney's step. His brisk pace catching the attention of an old gray cat with a mouse in its mouth and a guilty look on its face as it emerged from an alley to stare at him passing.

Musso caught up with him as he reached the precinct door.

"Mornin' partner."

"Mornin." Maloney acknowledged him with a nod, then they both greeted the desk sergeant without stopping. Straight to the breakroom, sparsely furnished with four white Formica tables, each with four white plastic chairs with chrome legs.The neon lights were too bright for comfort in the early morning . Smelling better than it tasted, the fragrant aroma of the coffee was misleading. Maloney took one sip. "I can't deal with this shit today."

"You're just jealous of those SWAT guys' coffee."

"Damn right I am. Golden boys, my ass. We should get as good as them. Let's go next door."

Musso didn't need much encouragement. The no-name-brand, Bronx establishment coffee shop a few steps down the sidewalk had much better coffee than the breakroom's offering and yet Musso wouldn't have to ruin his everyman, Brooklyn-born-and-bred, tough-guy image by going to a Starbucks. He'd never recover from the shame and indignity.

The storefront had been several other businesses through the decades before becoming a coffee shop. Twenty-foot-high ceilings covered in stamped tin, with insulated silver air ducts gave it an airy feel that belied it's small size. Stacked stone fronted the counter and covered the bottom quarter of the walls. It still bore features of the small bank it had been in one of its earlier incarnations: the former vault, now a private meeting room for customers' use. Best of all, though, the aroma of freshly ground coffee mixed with cinnamon smelled like Christmas. Definitely not a cookie-cutter establishment like Starbucks. Here, the workers did not wear uniforms and matching green aprons. Yet the crowd was every bit as diverse as the well-known chain—a mix of working stiffs, students and street people escaping the early morning cold.

Six customers stood on line to order and most of the tables were occupied, yet Musso found two seats at a small table while Maloney queued up.

Maloney brought the coffee over; both took it regular. The donuts he shared would have struck one as comical had any of the customers known they were cops. Maloney set his iPad on the table and said, "Keep an eye on it while I take a leak."

Musso grinned. "No sweat. I'll shoot anybody who even looks at it."

When he returned, Maloney said, " I see it's still there. Thanks."

"No problem. I only had to shoot one little old lady. You didn't hear it? It sure spiced up my day."

"You're a funny dude." Maloney added a couple of sprinkles of cinnamon to his cup from a small glass jar with a perforated green lid for Christmas, sitting on the table.

Musso tilted his coffee cup to his best friend. "Good idea, Partner. It sure beats the hell out of the crap at the precinct." He downed his donut in two giant bites, his cheeks puffed out like a winter squirrel's.

"No kidding. I bet—"

From the restroom hallway came a loud thud, interrupting him.

Maloney was on his feet in a flash, nearly colliding with an elderly woman who burst from the hallway running—if you could call it that; it was more of a shuffle. She stammered, "Somebody's hurt…In the men's room."

Musso put his shoulder against the door and shoved. After opening half a foot it stopped. He could make out dungaree-covered legs on the floor. "Sir? Sir?"

Getting no response, he and Maloney pushed harder against the door, slipping through the wider opening they created. Before them was a young man, likely a teenager, lying on the floor. An aerosol can of household cleaner sat on the cold tile next to him.

Musso shouted not at anyone in particular, "Dammit, call 911."

Maloney had his mobile out and was dialing before Musso finished the thought. Musso was on the floor, checking the young man's pulse and administering CPR when Maloney told him a wagon was on its way. Putting his ear to the young man's chest, Musso could hear his shallow, labored breathing.

The ambulance arrived in five minutes. That was one thing New

Yorkers were good about. They would do their best to get out of the way of emergency vehicles. Respectful of life *and* death. As two EMTs rolled a stretcher through the door of the coffee shop helpful citizens pointed out the way to the restroom.

Musso flashed his shield and told the lead EMT: "A kid, sniffing aerosol cleaner. He's breathing but unconscious."

Said Maloney, "Sucks to be him. Gonna wake up in the ER then be told he's under arrest.

Musso, "Stupid shits never learn."

Maloney shrugged. "We can always hope."

It wasn't that he was being unsympathetic but, knowing what his partner meant, Musso said, "We wouldn't have jobs if they did."

Chapter Five
Finding the Inside Man

Marquise chose his first candidate. Adonis was from the streets, seventeen, reed-thin, but with newly developing muscle, curly hair, and black-framed glasses. All the neighborhood girls thought him cute. He'd quit school in ninth grade but was street-wise.

He was picked up at his usual corner by Marquise and told that Zombies management wanted to talk to him about a new position.

He shuffled into the Valentine Street dining room, neither nervous nor nonchalant, just another day at the office. His personality helped him ace the interview. He sat at the table in an armchair and draped one denim-covered long leg over a wooden arm. All four liked Donnie, but two of them thought he was too young and, since he had to have a unanimous up-vote to be interviewed by Rev, it was a no-go for him.

Marquise told the next candidate, Georgie, he was being considered for a promotion or to have his territory expanded, made-up bullshit because Rev didn't want them to know the truth unless they were the one chosen. Georgie was twenty-one. Like Rev, a high-school football, baseball and basketball player, not good enough at any to play collegiately, but still a hero in the neighborhood. He'd pitched a no-hitter his senior season and threw twenty-one touchdown passes the same year. A shooting guard on the basketball team, he'd averaged twenty-three points a game during the winter. The only complaint: critics said the level of competition wasn't good enough.

After the four finished the interview all agreed he was ideal. Incognito had already vetted him, so he could be passed on to Rev for the final step.

Rev was added to the room to help maintain his anonymity and introduced as James.

"So how long have you been with us, Georgie?" he asked.

He shrugged. "Year and a half." Georgie would have been more respectful if he'd known who it was sitting across from him.

Less than five minutes later, Rev signaled Marquise, who said, "We'll make our decision and let you know."

"Aiight." Georgie stood and walked out without shaking hands or even thanking them.

After he left the room, Rev stood up and said, "He's not the one. Keep trying." Rev didn't say anything, but the truth was Georgie reminded him too much of himself when he was that age. He needed to learn situational awareness and respect to help him make better decisions. This mission was too important to give to someone who had poor judgment.

***

Leaving the office, Musso said, "I was thinking about going to The Pound. Wanna join me?"

His partner was always ready to go to the pound. "Yeah, I'll join you for a pint or two. Let me hit the head. I'll meet you there."

Musso gave him a thumbs-up as he held the door for Detective Sills, who was entering at the same time that Musso was leaving. He had to step to the side to let the large detective pass.

"Hey Big, you losing weight?" Calling him by his precinct nickname. Musso thought he looked like he'd lost a few pounds. Sills silently shook his head, not knowing if Musso was just busting his balls.

At five p.m. it was almost full dark outside.

"Bren, how youse doin?" Musso said, greeting his favorite bartender.

"Aces, Rock. How you doin'? The "how ya doins" made them sound like characters in a Budweiser Beer commercial.

Maloney, arrived and again, in an homage to his Irish heritage, ordered his usual Guinness. When the frothy mug arrived he sprinkled some salt in it to give it the thick head he liked, then tilted it toward Musso and to Brendan. "Cheers."

"Likewise," said Musso.

"Cheers," was the delighted response from Brendan, since most patrons didn't think to raise a glass to their bartender. It caused him to be thoughtful for a moment: "You know, I've been thinking about putting youse guys names on brass plaques on the backs of those two bar stools—just to commemorate, you know—youse being my best customers, for future generations. So, when the new young detectives come in, they know they have big shoes to fill."

Musso said, "That's cool, Bren. You should oughta do that. Just to let 'em know this ain't an easy job; we just make it look like it is."

Maloney just shook his head. From the jukebox nearby, Frank Sinatra sang "It Came Upon a Midnight Clear."

Beer foam blotting his untrimmed mustache, Maloney surveyed the dark bar. "You know, there are probably a dozen weapons in here. This has gotta be the safest bar in the city."

Musso nodded. "I know I feel safe."

Maloney used a handkerchief to wipe the 'stache. "I've been thinking about shaving this thing."

"You should. It looks like a goddamn Fuller Brush and you look like an 80s porn actor."

"That's not the first time you've said that and it's still isn't any funnier." Maloney looked at the unruly bristles in the requisite antiqued mirror behind the bar and shrugged to his reflection, turned around, tilted his mug at two rookies sitting in one of the booths lining the opposite wall, and said to Musso, "It sure doesn't take the new kids long to find this place, does it."

"Never. Proves they'll make good detectives. Shows the ability to sniff out leads."

One of the rookies was African-American and most people would think the other was some kind of Latino, but he was Filipino. He looked like an Asian Tom Cruise, especially in the teardrop sunglasses be wore in the dark bar at night. Neither looked old enough to legally drink beer, let alone be on the job.

"I've got an idea. You know how we wanted to find a new face—somebody young and unknown—to get inside the Zombies?" Maloney had been talking about it for the better part of a year.

"Yeah?

"It's possible we just found our men—euphemistically speaking—they both look pretty young."

Musso looked their way, nodded. "Let's mention it to the lieutenant.

"You know, we haven't seen them since their first day, when Lou gave them the tour," Maloney said. "I'm gonna go over and introduce myself."

Musso said, "Yeah, you do that. I'll stay here and watch how it goes, Musso said. "You know I don't talk to the new kids." He turned toward the small television above the bar that had been permanently tuned, at least since the nineties, to ESPN. It probably wouldn't broadcast anything else.

"Yeah, I know. You stuck up son of a bitch, you."

"I just remember how the old guys treated me when I was a rook. Just keepin' it real, payin' it forward." Young people's slang didn't work coming from the preternaturally uncool Musso,

Maloney sauntered over to the rookies, nodded and said, "John Maloney."

, "Antonio Hernandez," said the Filipino, "But you can call me Jun, short for junior."

"Morris Louis. Mo," said the African-American.

"Hey, welcome aboard."

"Thanks, we're glad to be here," said Louis.

Hernandez tilted his mug. "Cheers."

"So, what's your story?" Maloney wanted to find out for himself if they could do the job.

Louis said, "We met at the academy, different precincts for the past two years, got lucky. Both of us were recommended, passed the exam and we're back together again. Jun is the first in his family on the job. I'm second generation. My father walked a beat in midtown back in the day. He's tickled as shit I made detective."

"He should be. Quite an accomplishment at your age. You'll probably be commissioner by the time you're forty." Johnny grinned at him when he said it.

Louis took the good-natured jab graciously. "From your lips to God's ear," then took another swallow of beer.

"Me and my partner—that's him, the stoic son of a bitch over there at the bar—we got something we might could use your help on. Undercover, you know." Standing at the bar, Musso could tell they were talking about him but pretended not to notice. He stood straighter just to show a stiff upper lip. Had to do what he could to keep up his rep.

Hernandez looked interested for the first time. "Just let us know. That's what we're here for."

"Good to hear, I'll mention it to Lou. See what he says." Maloney turned. "Talk to you soon."

"Yeah man, let us know." Hernandez was getting pumped, anticipating some real police work.

Maloney turned to the side and shouldered his way in between two other detectives to reclaim his spot at the bar next to his partner. "So, Rock, Thanksgiving is next week. What are youse doing?"

"Ah, you know, with the kid away from home Rosalie and I will go to a hotel, chow down on a buffet."

"Man, to Hell with that. Youse guys aren't gonna eat any goddam rubber chicken and stovetop stuffing at any goddamn Holiday Inn. You're gonna have dinner with me and Mary Catherine. Turkey, stuffing, cranberries, sweet potato casserole, wine—the whole nine yards. We're family. You're supposed to be with family for the holidays."

"I'll have to confirm it with the boss, and wine makes me sweat, but sounds good."

"Okay, so let's make it happen. Create some memories."

"You want another pint?" Musso always wanted one more.

"I got time for another one."

"Good." Then to the man drawing their beers, "Brendan, two more." The bartender was stirring a drink with a long-handled bar-spoon, about the length of his forearm, twirling it like a baton. Working in a bar for almost two decades he'd had a lot of practice perfecting little moves like that one. He worked most nights and closed the Pound when he did. Because the South Bronx was a high crime area he was happy there were always cops around when he was locking up. A criminal would have to be insane to attempt an armed robbery. His gun would be outnumbered, probably less powerful than the ones he was facing down, and most likely he wouldn't be as accurate a shooter. He'd be a dead man walking.

Maloney, even though he was a Jets fan, they supported different teams, his partner pulling for their crosstown rivals and in reality John was jealous of their success. "Did you see the Giants game Sunday?"

"Yeah, But I don't want to talk about it. They just piss me off. Their damn defense hasn't been the same since Strahan retired."

"Ahh man, give 'em a break. It's hard to lose a Hall of Famer and keep playing like he's still on the defensive line. You know what they say about the D-line—overworked and underpaid.

"Underpaid, yeah right."

The bartender set down two cold beers on the bar before them. The moisture from the icy mugs left damp rings on the napkins. "Cheers."

"Thanks, Bren—to Strahan, God bless him," said Musso as he lifted his mug. The damp napkin stuck to the bottom, irritating him, and condensation poured down the sides of the heavy glass.

"To Michael," Maloney agreed.

"By the way, what'd you think of the kids?"

"Ah, you know youngsters. They want to change the world, do some real police work. But they seem okay."

"Well, maybe they'll get the chance."

"Maybe. Hard to believe we were that young once upon a time. At least I was. You came out of the womb old and crochety."

Musso made a face at that comment, although he knew there was a hint of truth to it. "Are you kidding me? You've got to be young and stupid before you can become this old and wise."

"Well, I for one intend to stay young at heart. Cheers," said Maloney, lifting his mug again.

Two pints turned into three and, before they knew it, they were the only ones left in the bar and Brendan was wiping it down, and putting away bottles of whiskey.

"We're gonna get outta your hair," said Carmine, looking apologetically toward Brendan.

"Yeah, next time, Bren."

"Don't youse forget where we are." Brendan knew he wouldn't have half the business he did if it weren't for the detectives from Fort Apache, and these two in particular.

"Never," said Maloney.

The bell over the door jingled when they exited the old Christmas bar into the wintery silent night. Snow had begun to fall while they enjoyed their pints. Noticing the white frosting when his best customers opened the door, Brendan called out, "Youse guys be careful of the ice." He'd have to shovel the sidewalk and throw salt on the entryway before he could open the next morning.

The quiet softness of the thick white blanket hushed the harsh sounds of the city. A mid twentieth century brightly lighted red-and-white barber pole stood in front of the shop next door like a peppermint stick peeking out of the snow at the North Pole.

It was the kind of enchanting night one could only find in New York City at Christmas. Colorful yuletide lights coloring the city and brightly shining stars draping the veil of darkness. Pretty, but this was still the New York City of noir crime. The grittiness lurked just under the festive holiday surface.

The street where Maloney lived was a mixed-use one, like nearly all streets in the Bronx—with offices, apartments, dry cleaners, cafes and bars. In a gentrified neighborhood in the Bronx or an exclusive one in a younger city it would be called a live, work, play community. John's building didn't have a hidden entrance, although it might as well have. An anonymous structure like a thousand others in the city. It had but two elevators. One used primarily for freight and he didn't like using it but tonight with a hand-lettered sign taped to the dull brass-colored door, the other was apparently out of service. Dark padding clad the attractive wood walls and a worn, stained, dark gray Berber carpet hid the shiny and bright light-colored marble tile. The elevator groaned from age and use. And strained to do its job. It would take over a minute for the ancient vertical conveyance to deliver him to his eighth floor apartment, and that was assuming nobody else interrupted the ascent. Maloney thought it was spooky and was glad he was armed, in case it wasn't just his imagination getting the best of him. Upon reaching its destination the elevator door bumped and hiccuped before it decided to open.

The lights were off in the apartment when he entered. When opened the door creaked as it swung wide. That sound was overtaken by the low hum of the refrigerator as he entered the combination family room and kitchen to the left. Slipping quietly through the arched doorway into the bedroom, he heard the pleasant mumble of Mary Catherine's soft, urgent snoring, which told him everything was okay, that life was good. She slept on her back and her shoulder-length blonde tresses formed a halo on the pillow around her head. One of her breasts had slipped out of the top of her nightgown and he resisted the urge to give it a squeeze, instead, straightening the neckline, covering her. He loved her apple-size breasts and it took all the self-control he could muster not to caress her even after nearly ten years of marriage.

She smelled of lavender, the fragrance of her bath soap. He smiled to himself at the thought of all the sweet-smelling bottles of lotions, gels, liquids and creams she brought home to make herself smell nice, her skin softer and her wrinkles smoother. Even if she did say she did it for him. He knew it wasn't true.

The warm glow of streetlamps sought solace through the bedroom window.

He undressed and showered, then shaved off his mustache by the light coming in the bathroom window so as not to disturb her, before he slipped quietly into bed.

In the dim light, she noticed what he'd done and caressed his face. "You shaved."

"Yes."

"You know the other detectives are going to give you grief…"

"Grief doesn't begin to describe it."

"Well, I like it. You're even more handsome."

"Thank you, babe. Their shit will be worth it, then. All that matters is what you think."

Mary Catherine whispered, "Did you have a nice time?"

"Yeah, babe. Absolutely. It's always good to spend time with Carmine away from the job. Speaking of that, I invited him and Rosalie to have Thanksgiving dinner with us."

"Good, great. You know I'll have plenty of food." Her tone was reassuring and comforting like a recording you hear on a phone.

"Yeah, I know. I live with you, remember? Carmine and I'll watch all the football we can stand. The Detroit Lions always host a game on Thanksgiving Day even though they suck pretty bad this year. Of course they nearly always suck. We'll watch it though, and any other games we can find."

"Well, Rosalie and I will want to watch the Macy's Thanksgiving Day Parade and *Miracle On 34th Street.*"

"Don't you worry your pretty little head about it. The parade is early and the games won't start until after the movie."

"Okay, baby. Night-night."

"Good night."

Before he closed his eyes, a toilet flushed in the apartment next door. The plumbing had been installed in the twenties and most of it had never been upgraded, accounting for the loudness. His neighbor, Mr. Kensil, was in his eighties and probably got up to urinate several times after his 9 p.m. bedtime. From talking with him in the elevator, John knew that he went to bed as soon as the reruns of *M*A*S*H** went off. He heard the sound of the elevated train and feared he'd be dodging it until daybreak.

***

After meeting in the break room and pouring their first cups of coffee Maloney and Musso strode to Lieutenant Michael Shapiro's office. They were on a mission and the lieutenant's door was open.

Maloney rapped twice on the open door beneath the small nameplate that announced the lieutenant to all, even though everyone in the precinct knew him and outsiders would most likely never gain entry into the inner sanctum. "Lou, you got a minute?" Maloney said before stepping into the office. He'd been annoying the hell out of the lieutenant since he came up with the idea months before.

A police supervisor and a typical New Yorker, always rushed for time. In answer to you got a minute? he said, "I've got thirty seconds. What's up?"

"You know Musso and I have been wanting to get someone on the inside of the Zombies."

"Yeah, you've been a royal pain in my flat ass. What about it?"

"Well, we were thinking about the new guys, Hernandez and Louis. They look younger than they are, about twelve. Nobody knows them on the street yet. What do you think about trying to get them in there? Carmine and I could run them, back them up."

"Might not be a bad idea. Let me sleep on it."

"Thanks, Lou. You won't regret it."

"Yeah, thanks." Musso was always the more laid back member of their team, but he thought it was a good idea, too. One of his better ideas. Although if his partner forced the issue he'd have to admit it was Maloney's brainstorm. Or else the younger detective might get his feelings hurt. He couldn't have that. Maloney had long been the more sensitive of the team.

***

The Zombies next candidate was Tommy, who was very cute and sweet. Tommy sang while he was dealing. He was old school, a Crooner on the corner who fancied the songs of Lou Rawls, Johnny Mathis and Nat King Cole. He emulated Lou's dramatic baritone to a T. His favorite song was the Rawls classic, "You'll Never Find Another Love Like Mine" even though it was recorded years before he was born. His was an old soul. People in the 'hood leaned out their windows just to listen to him sing. They thought of him as the neighborhood jukebox.

So even though everyone knew he was selling drugs they put up with it because they loved the free concerts.

With Marquis as his escort Tommy entered the dining room respectfully, without attitude.

Taking the lead, LT asked, "So, Tommy, what do you like about your job with the Zombies?"

Looking him straight in the eye, Tommy said, "The freedom, better than average earnings. I wish it carried better benefits, though. You know—health insurance, dental." He grinned at what he thought was a clever line. Indeed, he was a real charming kid.

"So what are your plans for the future?"

"I'm going to be on Broadway." Spoken not arrogantly, but confidently, matter-of-factly. If they'd known him better they would know he believed in the power of his thoughts and words and visualization. Although he never saw the champ fight due to his young age, he believed what Muhammed Ali was famous for saying: *"If the brain can conceive it and the heart can believe it, I can achieve it."* "Musicals. I'm a song and dance man."

Standing behind him, Marquise nodded. He'd heard him sing.

"But I'm going to finish school first. Get my degree. Major in musical theatre somewhere down south, where it's warm. The University of Georgia has a real good Fine Arts program. Take my moms with me. Get her out of the cold. The weather here is no place to live for someone who's getting older." Truth be told, moms was only in her early forties, but to Tommy that *was* old and she did look older than her years. To be fair to him, raising three kids on her own on the mean streets of the Bronx *had* aged her. And she had had the flu the previous winter, and since he didn't know much about things medical he worried that it could turn into pneumonia. He just knew people could die from the flu or pneumonia and it had scared him to death.

The four decided he was perfect. They asked Rev to come in and meet him.

"So, Tommy, tell me about yourself." Rev wanted to find out if he could think on his feet.

"There's not much to tell, sir. I just want to better myself, get my education and help my moms."

After a few more questions Rev finished with him and, being a very respectful young man, as he left the room, Tommy wished them all a happy Thanksgiving, knowing there would be nothing special about his. Chicken if they were lucky, stovetop stuffing and heat-and-serve rolls.

Marquise said, "He's great, isn't he."

Rev agreed. "A very polite, very respectful young man. Therein lies the problem."

Darelle said, "What do you mean?"

"He's smart. He has a future. I don't want to take that away from him. He needs to get out of this life, not get in deeper." Rev was in a hard business, a cold business, and he was a hard businessman. But he was also compassionate, and odd as it seemed in his chosen field, he cared about people.

"I need some time for reflection, to meditate," said Rev.

"Okay, boss. We understand," said Marquise. "We'll leave you alone,"

"No, no, no. I'm going home for a couple of days. I need to get away, be alone. Carmelito, can you drive me?"

"Sure thing, Rev. Any time you're ready." As the Zombies chief of security, Harry also acted as Rev's driver when needed. He stood, and interlaced his thick fingers, loudly cracking his knuckles.

"Let me grab a couple of things." Rev needed his journal. He wrote down his thoughts, ideas—about business, life, philosophy—things important to him. The journal was never far from his side. He didn't need it to function—he had an excellent memory—but he wanted a record of his thoughts.

It took about an hour in Incognito's Lexus luxury SUV. Not that far, but Bronx traffic was terrible.

Rev had an ulterior motive when he asked Harry to drive him. He wanted to pick his brain as they rode.

"So, Carmelito, do you think having someone on the inside would be a good idea? And don't agree with me just because you think that's what I want to hear. Tell me what you really think."

"Yeah, boss. I do, but the more I think about it I think it should be someone senior. But at the same time, we can't risk someone senior being on the inside."

"I've been thinking the same thing. I have to ponder this," he said with a pained look searing his face.

Incognito pulled up to the wrought iron gate that barred entry to the drive. Rev grabbed a device that looked like a garage door opener and and punched in a code known only to himself, his personal assistant and Caramelito and the double gates swung wide.

Pulling through, Carmelito took the circular drive and stopped at the double front doors to the Georgian-style mansion. Built in the sixties it had cost Rev millions. He remembered passing it on his bike when he was a kid and thinking, *I'm going to live in that house some day.* The innocent dreams of children.

Incognito escorted Rev to the entry and, unlocking the massive doors, they were greeted by Rev's large Rottweiler, Titan, who rose up and plopped his massive paws on Rev's chest. They covered each other with kisses.

"Good boy, Titan, good boy. Yeah, that's right. I love you, too. Okay, okay, that's enough," he said, extricating himself from the huge dog's show of love. Titan was Rev's second rotty. The first, Pearl, was a sweet girl but one with attitude. From their looks, people would think he had them for protection, but he liked rottys because of their sweet personality. They were a gentle, loving breed and he would never have anything but Rottweilers.

His staff—the housekeeper, a Chinese woman; and his personal assistant, an elderly African-American man who had been a close friend of his father's—had already decorated two Christmas trees, an enormous twelve-footer in the foyer—a stepladder they'd used to reach the upper branches still stood next to the large tree, it replacing a round table made of wood on which was displayed a large vase with an array of colorful flowers the rest of the year, and changed seasonally by the housekeeper, and a smaller seven-footer in Rev's library. Both were decorated with shiny, hand-blown Christopher Radko glass ornaments dusted in glitter. Rev loved Christmas and liked collecting the expensive European decorations. The scene—visible through the glass in the double front doors from the street, looked like a Norman Rockwell painting.

"If you don't need me for anything else I guess I'll be on my way, Rev. Let me know if I can do anything or if you just want me to take you back." He knew that Rev sometimes rode the subway just so he wouldn't forget his roots.

"Thanks, Carmelito. Will do." Although Rev was the only one that Harry allowed to call him by his Christian name, he couldn't get used to it. He preferred his self-bestowed name, Harry and he'd be back to Valentine before the working folks' lunch hours were over.

Rev took some logs from the copper holder on the hearth and placed them in the warm stacked-stone fireplace that covered one entire wall of the library. Books lined floor-to-ceiling shelves filling two walls; they surrounded the window looking onto the front lawn on the other. Philosophy, history, art and literature.

After lighting the kindling with a rolled up twist of old NY Times, Rev settled down at his desk as Titan curled up in front of it. Even though the large window was undraped little light entered because of the grayness of the skies. The flickering flames from the fireplace danced on the walls of the small room and washed Rev in a dim light that gave him a spectral appearance he would have liked had he been able to see his image. The light from a small shaded desk lamp illuminated his writing surface in the dim room to give it the same look.

It was in moments such as these that Rev sometimes thought that he'd like to give up the business, just stay here in the opulent luxury his illegal activities afforded him, but that was wishful thinking. The operation had grown too large; had taken on a life of its own, a living, breathing organism. Too many people depended on Rev for him to just walk away.

Rev leaned around the Christmas tree centering it to gaze out the picture window over the vast expanse of lawn to the Hudson River beyond. From his study and love of history he knew that in the early days of the country it had been known as the Broad River. The calm solitude he felt here, in his study, the antiquarian library, with his aged tomes and Titan, cleared his head and gave him clarity of thought.

The mansion was much the same as when it was built except for the passage behind one set of shelves on his library wall. A near hundred feet deep vertical passage with a steel ladder attached to the wall, descended to a maze of tunnels below the mansion, constructed by pirates centuries before. From his historical research Rev knew that in the bedrock beneath the Bronx was a labyrinth of tunnels from the Revolutionary War era and he only had to have a vertical shaft dug to connect to the maze. At the bottom Rev kept a Husqvarna 450 dirt bike that he could be astride in a little more than a minute, to beat a hasty exit if needed. Resting on its kickstand on the stone floor at the beginning of the maze of tunnels and he knew the direction to the soft slant of rocks on the east side of the Hudson.

Rising, he retrieved a bottle of de Montesquieu cognac and a small glass from its place on the shelf in the secret section. Returning to his chair the only sound piercing the diaphanous still of the room was the steady whisper of Titan's breathing.

Raising the snifter to his lips, he paused and closed his eyes—taking measure of the household. He knew the housekeeper was home; he could sense her energy even though she made not a sound. It was his gift. He first noticed it as a child. Ever since his youth he'd been in tune with his surroundings. Able to discern things that for others went unnoticed, hear sounds that most missed, perceive subtleties that the less nuanced couldn't. His maternal grandmother had had the same gift. That ability tied him to her in a way unknown by most with a generation of life separating them. He remembered when she was helping to potty train him he would perform for her even when he wouldn't for his mom. He felt his so-called telegnosis ability had served him well in his chosen career. Enabled him to hire people he could trust, stay away from those he couldn't.

Rev slowly reached for the journal in which he recorded his thoughts, from the place it always resided on the corner of his desk. A red cloth and gold brocaded volume he'd acquired in an Indian-Middle Eastern artifacts shop he'd stumbled across at Cannery Row on a visit to Monterey, California. The spine was worn from when Titan was a puppy, and during that rambunctious period, decided the volume would be worthy of a taste. The still visible teeth marks gave Rev a warm feeling with the memory.

Trying to get more money out of him, the proprietor of the shop said it was once owned by a famous Hindi who recorded the tenets of his religion within its pages. Rev didn't buy his grandiose tale, however, and offered the eastern man ten dollars. The proprietor couldn't say no to Alexander Hamilton, the only type of U.S. History he cared about—pictures of dead presidents and founders on small pieces of paper. Rev's already substantial ego growing with his financial success, he envisioned his writings as being important to future generations.

His thoughts returned to the petite glass of cognac and cupping the expensive crystal in both hands allow the blood coursing through his body to warm it, he sipped the clear amber liquid and alternated petting

Titan, while he wrote down the pros and cons of getting someone inside the NYPD. He thought, that the warm, silky smooth amber-colored cognac was, as the kids would say, the "bomb-dot-com-backslash-awesome, " and he laughed at the words. The distorted sound of his deep laughter echoed around him in the quiet of the oversize house and was slightly unnerving as it returned to him. Even Titan perked up his ears at the reverberation before it slowly died in the mansion's maze of halls. The ethereal silence of the house caused him to step over to his Bose stereo on the center shelf to turn on some Christmas music just so the sound of silence wouldn't be as overpowering.

A moment later his cell phone rang, interrupting his solitude with the sound of M.C. Hammer's "U Can't Touch This"—Marquise—a big fan of old school hip hop.

"Yeah, what's up?"

"The shipment will be at the next spot in the rotation at six."

"Ah, yes—the shipment." Rev mused, once again focused on the deadly serious business.

"Do we follow the usual plan, boss?"

"As long as it's working we keep using it."

***

The Second Group was a twelve-man squad that reported to Rev's four advisers and were serious muscle—or in this case, serious firepower—to discourage any of the competition to strike against them. A third group, even more lethal, would be hidden, providing more firepower in case the worst happened. These groups were not low-end street thugs. They'd been recruited from the military, private security firms and personal relationships with the Zombies leaders.

Rev knew the Russian mafia kept an eye on the Zombies and would love to hijack a shipment. And they were deadly; they'd think nothing of killing all of his top men to achieve their goal of ruling the NYC drug trade. In fact they'd probably love to kill all his top men.

Marquise sent a group text to the members of the two groups and within an hour all reported to the Valentine Street headquarters. Two o'clock. The shipment was due at the Hudson River dock at five. Plenty of time.

"Follow Harry downstairs and as usual he'll pass out the heavy equipment," Marquise told the group assembled in the parlor. The

Zombies kept their store of assault rifles in the basement in an impenetrable concrete saferoom reinforced with steel rebar. The men collected the proffered weapons, an assortment of AR-15s, 10s and less common semi-automatics, many of which were select fire from the gun makers or modified to full auto—and two magazines for each —A little overkill, yes —but better to have it and not need it than to need it and not have it.

As they made their way upstairs in pairs, and small groups, Marquise said, "All right men, let's roll." Most of them were hardcore vets of this kind of work, calm and relaxed, with the eye of the tiger.

Marquise had rented a plain white panel truck using a stolen credit card and a fake I.D. He had his go-to guy for such things make the I.D. to match the card. Marquise thought the man was as good at forgery as Frank Abagnale, the real-life subject of the Leonardo DiCaprio film *Catch Me If You Can,* and was considered the best in the city, which would also make him the best in the world.

The crew piled into the truck at the curb and, with Marquise driving under the speed limit, they moved toward the dock on the Hudson.

They usually picked up deliveries at one of the several marinas along the Hudson on the west side of the Bronx and Manhattan, not wanting to use the same one every time. They rotated between them all. Darelle had figured out a formula by which they alternated from marina to marina in a rotation that seemed to have no pattern, making it virtually unbreakable. Marquise had worked out a plan where an old friend of his who owned a small cabin cruiser would offload the drugs from a larger vessel from south Florida out in New York harbor, then bring the shipments to the selected marinas on the Hudson riverfront, not knowing which one until he received a call from Marquise, where the Zombies would take possession of them. It had worked well thus far.

The group arrived at a marina made up of a dozen piers each with expensive yachts of all sizes tied up in bays that looked like parking spaces. Incognito deployed the men, placing four of the best marksmen behind trees on the broad expanse of lawn sweeping down to the marina. Others were placed on yachts surrounding the slip where the yacht would moor with the illicit delivery. It wasn't long after everyone was in position that Marquise saw the *Pearl* 50-foot luxury yacht his friend bought with his proceeds from the illegal drug trade. A beautiful white cabin cruiser with gray accents, it had a maximum speed of 30 knots. The twin Volvo engines eased back and it approached the slip at a crawl. A lonely seagull soared on the cool drafts over the river and screamed at the men as if warning them to be watchful.

As Marquise gave his friend a wave indicating it was safe to dock, three Caucasians clad in work coveralls and pushing gray plastic trashcans on noisy wheels rolled down two of the piers. The November wind off the river chilled Marquise to the bone, but the garbage men didn't wear jackets in the late autumn cold, ensuring their coveralls remained visible as if they wanted to appear to be something they weren't. As they neared Marquise, each withdrew an assault weapon from his bin. But Incognito's men were paying attention and had been well trained. Before the intruders could even raise their weapons, the Zombies marksmen cut them down in an avalanche of automatic gunfire.

***

"Maloney, Rocky, everybody goddammit, heads up. A well-meaning concerned citizen, God love him, just called from El Marina. Said it sounds like the 4th of July on fast forward over there. Everybody on deck. Roll 'em. I'll let your buddies at ESU in on the deal. Youse can meet them there."

Carmine said, "Shit, I thought we were going to have a whole day without any action."

"Wishful thinking, Rock."

"I can hope, can't I?"

All the detectives from Fort Apache raced toward the docks. As they neared the waterfront, a plain white panel truck rolled slowly toward them; at the same time an expensive yacht was pulling languorously away from the marina. It had all the signs of a peaceful early evening on the river in the Bronx.

***

Marquise willed himself not to speed as he drove north on the Hudson River road toward Valentine: "Damn, cops," he muttered as a squadron of unmarked police cars raced toward him.

Wouldn't do to be pulled over with a truckload of men with

automatic weapons.

***

Carmine and John were anxious to get the new guys on the street and infiltrate the Zombies.

On the way in to work Johnny stopped at the coffee shop and got the lieutenant an eggnog latte. Figured buttering him up with a warm Christmas drink on a cold morning couldn't hurt. The thought crossed his mind that he would've liked to get him a hot-buttered rum but, it was too early in the morning—and even in this day and age, drinking on duty was still frowned on.

Peering through the large window into the boss's office, Johnny saw he was talking to Louis and Hernandez. Maybe something was in the works.

Walking away from the office Johnny bumped into Carmine. "Morning, partner."

"Mornin, sunshine. That for me?" Carmine was staring greedily at the cup containing eggnog latte.

"I wanted to butter up Lou, but Louis and Hernandez are in there, so I guess you can have it. Don't want it to get cold."

Carmine didn't say anything. Just gave a grateful shrug and took the offered drink.

"That was the shit yesterday afternoon, wasn't it?" Carmine had a way with words, brief and to the point. Thirty-five years on the job had taught him to be concise.

"Yeah, three bodies dressed in work overalls with automatic weapons."

"You can bet your ass the Russians had their hands in it."

"I wouldn't take that bet. Afraid I'd lose."

The next morning dried brown bloodstains and empty shells covered the piers and the grassy lawn fronting El Marino, the area marked off by yellow police tape. The normally peaceful neighborhood was tainted by the smell of death.

Chapter Six
Battles

Harry and Marquise regretted killing the interlopers. The whole thing smelled of the goddamn Russians. The dead had been beefy, middle-aged Caucasian men covered in prison tattoos; they were definitely old school, those who thought nothing of taking what they wanted and using any means available to get it. Deadlier than people watching the news on television could imagine in their wildest nightmares.

Although the Zombies had been able to turn the tables on them, Harry and Marquise could see how this wouldn't end well for anyone. Nobody wanted the Russians to gain a foothold in the Bronx. They didn't want just the drug trade. They prostituted teenagers and murdered for hire. They had no scruples at all while the Zombies were a known commodity focused on only one thing.

***

As expected the Russians were pissed that failure had cost them three of their top shooters. Stone cold killers were hard to find. You couldn't just put an ad in the *New York Times*. The Moscow Times maybe, but Moscow was half a world away.

"How could you *zadrotas* fuck this up?" Arkady Varushkin's lieutenants were literally scared to death of his wrath and knew that he really didn't want an answer and it would be best if they didn't reply.

He yelled at the low-level worker who brought in coffee. "I'm hungry. Go get me some goddamn *havak*." Most of the men wore black polyester pants and shirts, except for the man delivering coffee who wore a lightweight cheap Hawaiian shirt. Coming from Russia he didn't know they were worn primarily in Hawaii and maybe Florida—not New York City—and definitely not in winter.

"What do you want, sir?"

"Anything, just some god-damn *havak*, American fucking food."

"God-damn *Zadrota*. Fuckin' moron. Why can't I find good help?" He asked rhetorically of no one.

"And yesterday, the black fuckin' *Amerikosys*. We lost three of our best men. Payback's going to be a son of a bitch. We'll bide our time, I'll decide when the time is right and then we're goin' to take out every last one of those fuckin' Amerikosy black sons of bitches. Next time we're going to *tibrit* all their drugs and their goddamn *hrusky*. They won't have a single George Washington left when I finish with them. Fuckin' Zombies. I'll show them goddamn zombies."

His iPhone rang and he couldn't find it. "Where is my goddamn *jablofon*?"

Finally locating it in a desk drawer, he answered. One of his lower-level minions. "Yeah, the fuck you want? You dumb shits fucked up. You'll be lucky if I don't slit all of your goddamn throats. And forget this number. I'll call you if we need to talk. Fuck," he shouted. "I'll go back to mother-fuckin' Russia before I put up with this shit any longer." He didn't really mean it because he'd have no life in the motherland, but none of his people knew he was putting on an act for them.

Act or not, they had never seen him this pissed before, however. Vasily had been with him for four years, handpicked by the higher-ups in Mother Russia to be their eyes and ears on Varushkin and he couldn't wait to report this to the higher ups. It might mean he'd get to replace him. This was a huge error on Arkady's part.

But it would also serve to motivate him…and make him even more dangerous.

***

"I think we got off easy," Rev said to his advisors.

Harry said, "I think you're right, Rev. We could have lost some good men and a bunch of product if we hadn't been prepared."

"You guys deserve the credit for that," said Rev. He believed in giving praise to his inner circle and rewarding them with money in addition to the recognition.

"And we need to be ready. Since we killed three of theirs I'm sure they'll be wanting to retaliate, have a visceral need, to retaliate." Rev didn't get where he was by not thinking ahead.

"But they came after us. Why would they want revenge for what they did?" LT was thinking fairly and not realistically. His only job was being the Zombies' attorney. Killing and revenge was not something he had a lot of experience with.

Harry said, "It doesn't matter who started it. 'An eye for an eye.' "

With his self-proclaimed connection to la Cosa Nostra, Harry understood that biblical passage better than most.

"You're right, Carmelito," Rev said, "That's why we'll have to be ready for them. I don't think they'll hit us right away. I suspect they'll try to lull us to sleep—hope we forget about it, then attack us when they *think* we'll least expect it."

Harry said, "So it's up to us to expect it when they do it."

"Exactly."

***

The lieutenant walked into the squad room. Using his stage voice, he said, "Musso and Maloney—in my office. Now."

They followed him as if they were on a mission.

"Sit."

They did as commanded.

"I'm ready to pull the trigger on getting the new guys into the Zombies. Maybe we could have headed off that disaster yesterday if they'd been in there."

"Great. Thanks, Loo." Maloney had wanted this for a while.

"Yeah, thanks." Even though he didn't sound like it, Musso was enthusiastic about it also. He never sounded enthusiastic.

"Well, go out with them. Get them on the street. Work it the way you think is best. Just get them in there."

"Will do," Musso said. To Maloney: "Let's go talk to them."

Walking into the squad room, Musso said, "Hernandez, Louis, let's go get some coffee."

They got up from their desks without a word. They were expecting this after the lieutenant's talk with them. He had already broken the news.

They turned toward the break room. Maloney said, "No, let's go get some real coffee."

Musso said, "I'll get the car."

The other three waited in front of Sergeant Cabrera's massive desk just inside the lobby. Too cold to wait outside but not really warm inside due to the doors opening and closing. The gray skies shrouded the Bronx and fog hung low obscuring the houses across the street. The light rain made it feel colder than the mid-30s it actually was. Musso pulled up out front and they hurried to the car.

Musso had to be careful to watch for brake lights ahead of him in the dense fog.

"Thanks for giving us this chance," said Louis.

"Yeah, we're grateful," said Hernandez. "We know it was your idea."

"No problem. But let's don't get all touchy-feely," said Musso. He wasn't the type to show his feelings except with his daughter. She could melt his heart. Sick with pneumonia as a toddler, she wasn't expected to see her first day of primary school. But Anjelica was now a twenty-six year old Italian-American beauty. And Musso still didn't like guys coming around to, as he put it, *court* his little girl. He had scared more than a few suitors by sitting in the living room and feeling the need to clean his service weapon at the very moment a young man showed up.

"Let's go to that coffee shop that just opened on Westchester," said Maloney.

"That'll be good," Musso. "We shouldn't go next door. Might be some of our brothers there. Don't want any of them to find out yet. The walls have ears, you know."

Except for the sound of static and intermittent interrupting messages from the radio, they rode the rest of the way in silence.

Parking the unmarked cruiser in a no-parking zone, Musso retrieved the laminated NYPD parking pass from the glove compartment and placed it in the cruiser's dash. He lit a cigarette before exiting the car. He'd smoked thirty years before but he'd recently picked up the habit again. Saying it calmed him, he blamed the stress of the job. And Rosalie was giving him hell about it. She'd said, 'I don't want to bury you. I want you to grow old with me. He thought of that and after taking two drags his conscience got the better of him and he tossed it in the street.

The smell of saltwater and sea air was fresh in the early morning. It was present anywhere one went in the Bronx. It was the only one of the New York City boroughs not on an island, but on the mainland; however it had salt water on three sides and therefore salty air enveloping it. The sidewalk was brisk with pedestrian traffic; everyone bundled up against the cold during the early-morning rush to work. They shouldered their way past a group of smokers, drawing indignant looks from them. Trash collectors dropped a loud plastic bin to the concrete, startling several of the group. One lone man negotiated a motorized wheelchair against the detectives' pace. Another stood at the corner speaking loudly and gesturing wildly even though they couldn't make out what he was saying. Back in the day, Musso would have thought him one of the city's thousands of mentally afflicted homeless. Now instincts and experience told him it was a boss yelling at an employee or a husband yelling at his wife hands-free from his smartphone. The man turned his head and, seeing the earbud in the opposite ear, Musso knew he'd guessed right. They dodged piles of trash on the sidewalk in front of each of the small businesses along their walk, confronted by on-rushing heads-down commuters and, even though it was early morning, a delivery man pushing a hand truck laden with six cartons of beer for the lunch hour. The smell of vehicles exhaust fouled the air, while a roaring Delta jet taking off from nearby LaGuardia and making conversation impossible, banked south and passed in front of the still visible early-morning moon. To Musso it was all part of the lyrics in the the city's song. His was an old soul and the melody of the traffic, horns bleating, the voices on the sidewalk and jetliners departing, were all part of the refrain that made New York New York.

The nondescript building that had been home to many other businesses in the previous century wore a yellow neon sign proclaiming "Wake The Dead Coffee Shop," the only indication of its current purpose. Another neon sign flashed "Open". Next-door was an adult gift shop and video store that appeared to be on the verge of being driven out of business by the anonymity of and the easy availability of Internet porn. Musso saw the porn shop and thought, "*Sick sons-of-bitches*". He didn't understand how a normal red-blooded American male would rather look at pictures or videos than have a real woman. Down an alley, between the adult store and the coffee shop, a man urinating on the brick wall—showing no embarrassment or fear of harassment—eyed them as they passed. In one of the world's largest cities that was such a common occurrence most policemen didn't take notice. So many millions, so few public restrooms, and the call of nature so strong, law enforcement tried to be understanding as long as people were discreet about it.

As they neared the entrance of the new coffee shop an exiting customer opened the door and the warm aroma of fresh ground beans brewing greeted them even before they entered. A blazing fire laid in a fireplace with a hammered aluminum surround dominated the main room, providing warmth against the stinging cold of the late November morning, but the steady stream of customers opening the door allowed the chill to invade the otherwise warm room. Ceramic skulls on the mantle seemed a little out of place, but it didn't seem to bother the customers, as a half dozen people were online ahead of them. The front of the bar was clad in aluminum that matched the fireplace surround. It smelled the same as all coffee shops—the intoxicating aroma of fresh, hot coffee. The fragrant smell of coffee killed the odor of the Bronx. There was a reason the salespeople at department store cosmetics counters offered customers coffee beans to inhale between trying different colognes and perfumes. It was effective at killing smells.

"Let me have one of those cranberry oat bars," ordered Musso, to go along with his large dark roast regular coffee after looking over the glass case filled with freshly prepared pastries. Glad the local shop eschewed the fancy names like grande and venti that Starbucks made popular, he wouldn't have used them anyway. Taking a large swallow, and as usual enjoying the opportunity to embolden his tough guy image, while smacking his lips, Rocky said, "That's a damn fine cup of *Shut The Hell Up.*"

Maloney got a cranberry orange croissant to go with his non-fat latte', way-too-sweetened with three stevias. His sweet tooth was working overtime this morning.

The shop was ready for Christmas with pairs of foot-tall silver and gold trees on most tables and counters.

The male barista looked like a young Russell Crowe. The women customers liked his dimples. The crevices looked like a combination of Crowe's and a young Tom Selleck's. He wore a small diamond stud in the topmost point of the left canyon. A man in a gray uniform walked in delivering a fresh supply of towels and he and the barista greeted each other by name, obvious to an observant detective that the towel man had been on the route for a good while.

The rookie detectives pushed two butcher-block tables together for the four of them to sit around. The screeek of the tables scraping across the tile floor would have awakened the dead. Someone listening would have imagined an opening crypt. Colorful primitive art and posters of rock concerts from the sixties, including one from the nearby

Woodstock Festival, haphazardly decorated the blood-red-toned walls. Standing by, nursing his dark roast regular coffee, Musso noticed an attractive young woman paying for her coffee. Slender, dressed in painted-on jeans, a skin-tight, purple, v-neck top and a vest that looked like it had been sheared from a wildebeest. It was obvious to a well-trained detective's eye that her's were large, man-made breasts. She withdrew a wad of ones from the pocket of the vest, from which she peeled off six to pay for her latte.' Being the astute, veteran detective he was, and noticing her large breasts and the single dollars she used for payment he deduced that she was a dancer paying for her drink with tips from the previous night's lap dances. She probably hadn't been off work long after dancing the midnight-to-eight shift at one of the cities' many gentlemen's clubs. "Say Something", a sad song by Christina Aguilera with A Great Big World, was playing on the stereo providing background music and Musso noticed a tear well up in the white of her eye. She withdrew a tissue from where she had pulled out the ones and wiped her right eye, then the left one, for good measure. A sensitive lady.

When Musso returned to the group, Maloney, noticing the scene with the young lady, said, "I wonder how old she was when her titties came in."

Musso said, "Probably about twenty-six, twenty-seven" He'd seen them up close and personal and was the more cynical of the duo.

Agreeing, Hernandez said, "No shit."

Maloney said, "Good one, Rock. So up close it's obvious they're fake?"

Musso said, "Hell, I'd have been able to tell they were fake from twenty miles away.

Maloney looked through a doorway and pulling back a curtain draping the opening, said, "Hey, there's a sofa and leather chairs in here if you guys want to be more comfortable."

" I'd rather be warm. Let's stay by the fire." said Musso, when what he really wanted was to stay where he could continue to eye the dancer.

Louis picked up a book from a shelf containing popular hardbacks mostly from the twentieth century. "Look, my favorite Christmas novel of all time, *Catcher In The Rye*." Holden Caufield kills me."

"Very funny," said Hernandez. He knew that that was what Holden said about his kid sister throughout the famous novella. He'd read a volumn published in Spanish when he was a kid in the Philippines.

Wanting to get them focused, Musso said, "Yeah, so you know what we want," said Musso. "We want somebody—you two—on the inside of the Zombies."

Maloney said, "Yeah, who knows—maybe we could've headed off that gun battle yesterday if we'd had you guys in there."

Louis said, "The brother and the Pinoy, we can handle it."

Musso said, "Pinoy?"

Louis said, "Another word for Filipino. Jun taught it to me."

Hernandez asked, "So where do we go in?"

As the senior detective, Musso took control. "We figure you'll have to go in as common street dealers."

Maloney jumped in. "But we suspect you hotshots—as sharp as you guys are—you'll be management in no time."

Hernandez and Louis knew he was just giving them the business. They could take it, though. NYPD detectives learned to develop thick skin fast.

"Yeah, and we might be the boss of youse guys before we're done," Hernandez said, and Louis fist bumped him.

Musso and Maloney ignored that comment. They'd had young, inexperienced guys as their supervisors before. Neither wanted that again.

The hot coffee and caffeine got the cops' testosterone flowing and Musso started telling stories from back in the day. The tales just made him sound old to the kids.

Maloney said, "Rocky's not as old as he sounds. It just comes across that way since he was here for 9/11, the Preppie Murder case, even Son of Sam," He hesitated, then added, "Come to think of it, he *is* an old bastard."

They all laughed at that, including Musso. Even he had to admit that was a funny line.

"Hey, hey now, I wasn't here for Son of Sam. I'd have to be seventy years old."

"Well, I thought you were," said Maloney.

"Shit. Come on now. You're gonna hurt my feelings." There was no way anybody was going to hurt Musso's feelings—Italian tough guy, a former Golden Gloves boxer, NYPD boxing champion. If he hadn't become a cop he might have been in la Cosa Nostra. The only feelings he had were for his family and his partner.

They discussed the details of the plan. Musso and Maloney would run the operation. How and how often they would be in contact and what to do if they needed the NYPD to bail them out, were ironed out over more coffee.

"So, when do we start?" asked Louis.

Drawing it out, between sips, Musso said, "You should probably get out on the street...hang out on the corners where the dealers are...be noticed."

***

The following morning Louis and Hernandez went undercover. The brother and the Filipino looked like a Starsky and Hutch for the younger generation. They separated, each making his way to the Zombies prime corners by different routes. Taking their time. Casual-like. Like they had no where they had to be. Being noticed.

Of course hanging out on street corners was nothing new for Hernandez. He'd done it for years as a kid in Manila. He'd even surprised himself that he hadn't ended up in prison. Hadn't killed someone or been killed, when he was young and stupid. His grandmother, the matriarch of the family, called Nanay in Filipino families, thought Jesus had performed a genuine miracle because of her pleas to the Blessed Virgin. Like many Catholics she knew that no good son would turn down a request from his mother, and Jesus was the best son of all.

Bodegas, off-track betting offices, phone booths from a different era and mom-and-pop restaurants dotted the landscape. An hour later they converged on the opposite side of the street, walking west from Ft. Apache toward Valentine Street. When they spotted a crowd on a street corner they knew they were in the right place.

They spied the dealer. The salesmen didn't even attempt to disguise what they were doing. They'd have to separate again so they wouldn't be spotted together.

Louis said, "I think this looks like my kind of place," and he turned toward a stoop and plopped down on the steps to perch.

As Louis peeled off, Hernandez stepped up to the open window of a bodega and got an "everything" bagel and a coffee, "regular."

"How do you want your coffee?" he asked Louis in an outside voice.

"Just like me, dude—strong and black." He grinned as he said it. "I need the caffeine to fuel my aggression."

Jun brought over the styrofoam cup filled with hot coffee to his partner and best friend, then strutted up the street reminiscent of the John Travolta character, Tony Manero, walking down a Brooklyn street eating his three stacked slices in *Saturday Night Fever*. Louis blew on the hot coffee to cool it and just shook his head at his best friend and looked away.

Six short blocks north and one wide one east, Hernandez slowed his stride. There were several people at the corner he was approaching. Reminded him of days back in the 'hood. Instinct honed on the street told him it would be one of the Zombies' best corners for business.

Two young teenagers were passing a basketball between themselves just feet from where he passed. He intercepted the ball.

"Hey man, that's our ball. Give it back." It was a ratty, no-name, rubber b-ball for use on concrete and beat-up macadam.

Hernandez said, "I don't want your sorry-ass ball. Just wanted to see if you had any game." Filipinos loved American basketball and even though most of them aren't tall enough for the sport some of them had pretty good ball skills. Hernandez wound up to throw the ball at one of the kids and dropped it behind his back and caught it with his off-hand just to mess with the truant. All the time watching the dealer out of the corner of his vision.

Continuing nearer to the corner, he and the dealer locked eyes. A bad error on his part. Hernandez didn't want the dude to even notice him the first day. Oh well, he'd recover. He didn't acknowledge the dealer at all, not with an eye twitch or even an arch of an eyebrow. He could play the game with the best of them. He remembered studying Frank Serpico, in the academy; the best undercover detective in NYPD history and how he not only dressed when undercover, but how he acted, how he ate, how he wouldn't take showers or even brush his teeth, totally immersed in the character. Jun might be a rookie detective but this was his big chance to show what he could do and he would not blow it.

Kept walking, taking note of the surroundings—the customers, the neighbors and neighborhood—blending in, convincing himself that it would be a good place to start his act.

In the meantime, Louis had a different plan. Approach the street corner dealer he'd spotted and, after a little small talk, ask how he could get a job. He heard the dealer singing. The kid had a great voice, but he stopped as detective Louis got closer.

Louis smelled the sickeningly sweet cheap cologne the dealer wore hanging heavy on the air.

"Hey dude how's it going? Whyn't you introduce me to your sister?"

"My sister's eleven."

"Too bad. What'da they call you? And…how's a brother get a gig like this?"

"Name's Tommy. You got to be smart, have a head for business, be charming—like me, and most importantly know somebody."

"I know somebody."

"Who you know?"

"Know plenty of people—my moms, my cousins, brothers in the 'hood."

"Gettin' tireda your shit, man."

"I'm cool, dude. I'm cool." The dealer's push back made Detective Louis worry that he might have come on a little too strong. Oh well.

"I don't see nobody cool."

"Well, I'll check you later. I got some stuff I gotta take care of." And he strutted off.

"Take your time," Tommy said to the back of Louis' head.

Chapter Seven
The Plan

A plan was beginning to crystalize for Rev. He didn't have the details figured out yet, but it was audacious and, assuming it worked, he would learn everything the pigs knew about the Zombies. He prided himself in being ballsy and taking risks—calculated risks had helped him to accomplish all he desired and provided him with life's dreams.

It would be different this time, though. He couldn't tell anyone what he had in mind. He knew they wouldn't support him, but he was still the boss and sometimes he had to make decisions without consulting his advisors, just to prove to them that he would. Usually he like to get a consensus among them before implementing a plan, but this time he was going out on his own. It seemed that he was guided by a greater being, an unseemly force that he had to answer to more than his four advisors. And sometimes he had to keep his own counsel just because he could.

***

Louis and Hernandez didn't talk until their return to Fort Apache. Didn't want their targets to see them together.

They felt good about their plan and knew it was just a matter of time until they both had their own corners and were in business.

"So how'd you do?" Hernandez asked his buddy.

"Dude was a little skittish. I had to give him some space. But it's cool. In a couple of days he'll be begging me to join. Once he sees how clever, charming and smart I am."

"Yeah, that oughta do it," Jun said, rolling his eyes. Even he could take only so much of Louis' shit.

"Okay, big man, how'd it go for you?" asked Louis.

"I'm hanging back, gonna let him approach me," said Hernandez. He had patience and could work without being rushed. He knew the greatest of all detectives, Frank Serpico, said that the most important attribute an undercover detective could have was patience.

"Let me know how that works out for you."

"Will do, buddy."

"So wanna hit the Pound, again?" said Louis.

" Let's do it. Anne's going to forget she has a boyfriend, but she'll get over it. She's already pissed at me for not showering or brushing my teeth." Jun had been with Anne for over two years, and he was planning on giving her a ring for Christmas, a little more than a month away. Two months' salary for an engagement ring was going to kill him. He wondered who decided that shit, anyway. For a newly-minted NYPD detective third-grade it would amount to over $11,000.00

"Well, I'm not too happy about it myself and I'm not even sleeping with you."

"To be honest with you, she hasn't been sleeping with me much lately, either."

"TMI, partner."

The Dog Pound was quickly becoming their favorite place. Close to the job, plus they enjoyed hanging out with their brothers and sisters in blue when off the clock.

They slid into a booth and the one server on duty, Marcela, although all the regulars called her Marcie, strolled over, peacocking for the newly christened detectives. Blonde with blue and green streaks in her hair, as she walked, she flashed dimples so deep you could hide a one-carat diamond in each. They framed a crooked mischievous smile. Her earrings looked like a mountain climber's carabiners. But once you noticed the large tattoo of an eye on the inside of her right bicep you were unable to notice anything else. The slight stutter when she spoke would be described by most of the male patrons as cute. She'd had the stammer since she uttered her first word. A smartass by nature, her intuition always told her when the newbies arrived. What she said was they were still wet behind their ears and needed somebody to teach them the ways of the world. She called them all sweet pea and usually volunteered her services, but as yet no one had taken her up on her offer. A damn shame. She knew she could show them a thing or two, But they would have thought their mom's best friend was hitting on them even if they did think she was a "milf".

Louis and Hernandez both ordered a Sam Adams Harvest Pumpkin Ale. It was only sold during the fall, so they wanted to take advantage of its seasonal availability. The tabletop on which they propped was scarred with decades of forgotten graffiti from different eras and the initials of those for who now didn't even offer memories to the ones who etched them into the surface.

In the booth behind them sat either an aging rock star or an equally old former vice detective, with long silver hair pulled back in a pony tail, a silver beard and wearing tortoise-framed, dark sunglasses at night, so no one could be sure exactly, which he had been.

Detectives Musso and Maloney had had a slow day. Decided to cap it off with a quick pint.

Pretending not to have noticed them until the older detectives reached the booth where the rookies sat, Hernandez said, "Hey, quit talking about them. It's the old guys...er, I mean, the senior detectives, er, uh-oh."

Musso said, "I'll give you the benefit of the doubt and pretend like I didn't hear that and that you really didn't say it."

"Thank you, Mr. detective...Rock...er, sir, sorry sir. Just a slight slip of the tongue. I don't even know how it happened." Although Filipinos loved boxing and they all thought they were the next Manny Pacquiao, Hernandez wouldn't have wanted any of Musso in or out of the ring.

***

It appeared that due to the approaching holidays, the criminal element seemed to be taking a break. Hernandez and Louis hadn't yet found the opportunity to infiltrate the Zombies and Musso and Maloney were not as busy as usual.

The Russians didn't know the meaning of rest, however. Arkady was having planning meetings. He didn't even understand himself, why he was so driven to wipe out the Zombies. It seemed to be more than just getting rid of the competition. He seemed to have a visceral desire to kill them all, and he didn't know exactly where it was coming from. It felt like someone on the outside was controlling him. Although not known for his intelligence, he was diligent and made sure he was well prepared for most situations. And he and his crew were planning an attack—striking back at the Zombies and hitting them hard. But for now they would bide their time, making sure the element of surprise was their friend. They would not rush into this thing.

They sat around a scarred wood table in a makeshift conference room in a corner of an unheated, filthy warehouse. One of the group, bored, used a pocket knife to carve Cyrillic characters into the surface in front of where he sat.The smell of rubber, grease, oil, damp concrete and sweat hung on the dead air like a wet blanket. A pile of worn-out car and truck tires was piled in the opposite corner. Weapons lay stacked in the center of the table, just in the event they might be needed. Kalashnikovs, the most widely used rifle in the world and, according to many military men in virtually all countries, the best, and Tokarevs. The Russians were old school and if they could help it wouldn't use weapons that weren't made in the motherland. They were a rough-looking group. If you saw any one of them approaching you on the sidewalk, you'd cross to the other side of the street.

Sentries flanked the roll-up metal door that opened to the sidewalk. Arkady and his crew did everything possible to be invisible, but they couldn't know for sure if word had gotten out or not, about their meeting and they obviously were on edge.

Arkady's grim face spoke volumes. "Listen up, you sons-of-bitches," he said and all of them—middle-aged Caucasians who looked used-up, most of them in their forties, each of them looking at least a decade older than their actual ages, literally snapped to attention.

There was no doubting Arkady's anger. The evil in his eyes held a look of permanence none of them had ever seen before. No one at the table was under the mistaken impression they were his friend. They were his henchmen, his minions. They did his bidding, and if they didn't, their heads would be cut off—figuratively and literally.

"We have to avenge our comrades. By making an example of the fucking Zombies we will send a message to the fucking pasta-eaters, the rice eaters and the goddamn cigar-rollers. They will not fuck with me."

He had made it personal because he knew if he didn't avenge the death of his three men—if he didn't retaliate, hit back and hit back hard—the real bosses, the ones he answered to in Russia, would have his head, or worse, send him to Siberia. Which even though that was his home, the idea of it was unthinkable. He couldn't leave this country. As cold as it was in New York, it wasn't as cold as Siberia, and besides, he couldn't leave his spicy Colombian girlfriend. The first time he met her in one of the city's best dance clubs, he told her she was hot and she said *I'm not hot. I'm spicy.* He couldn't believe his good fortune in meeting her. Fifty years old, but typical of Latinas and Asians, looking twenty years younger, Nora Rodriguez kept him warm at night. And he just enjoyed the hell out of looking at her in the short, low-cut, skin-tight dresses she preferred. He kept her closet filled with Jimmy Choo stilettos and poured her all the Prosecco she could drink and she was happy—and she kept him happy. Relieving his pent-up stress whenever he needed was all he required—that and being arm candy at a moment's notice.

No one said anything. They were there to listen. His advisors didn't advise. They knew his position was tenuous. He didn't want their counsel. He wanted them as a sounding board. And it wasn't that they were that loyal to him, but they didn't know who his replacement would be. It was just—the devil you know...

The meeting over, Arkady said, "*Dos vedanya.*" Have a nice day. He always minded his manners, even if he was an asshole.

Chapter Eight
The Holidays

Mary Catherine began her cooking on Wednesday morning. Starting before Johnny even left for work, the apartment already smelled succulent. The stuffing was from an old New England recipe that included pecans and crumbled Italian sausage. It was Johnny's favorite holiday dish and she delighted in cooking it for him. But he loved everything she made, the cranberries, broccoli-rice casserole, green bean bundles soaked in Russian dressing and especially her sweet potato casserole. Covered with marshmallows, pecan pieces were like buried hidden treasures within.

As Johnny made his way to the door, a jacket over his shoulder and his weapon on his hip, he stuck his finger in the marshmallow topping, and giving it a lick, said, "Yum-yum."

MC pointed toward the door with a wooden spoon and said, "Out."

He wagged his finger at her. "This is torture. I can't believe you're making me wait until tomorrow."

Shaking her head at him, like he was a child, "Out," she repeated, in feigned anger.

***

Maloney knew he could get away with being a few minutes late. As long as he made Lou's meeting at ten he'd be good. He'd be there by three minutes after eight as long as he didn't run into any bad guys mugging old men or any pros that needed rousting. Either of those events would slow him down.

He encountered no bad guys that needed arresting or little old ladies who needed help crossing the street, so he made it with time to spare.

***

The lieutenant had called a 10:00 meeting just to keep the troops on their toes. He knew there wasn't much happening on the streets so he wanted to keep them busy, didn't want them to lose their edge. The day before, Tuesday before Thanksgiving, there had been less traffic on the streets already. Today, Thanksgiving Eve, the Bronx was a ghost town, unlike Manhattan, which was already getting crazy, however, with out-of-towners arriving for the Macy's Thanksgiving Day Parade. The NYPD knew all the hotels were at capacity and they knew they had to be visible, make their presence known not only to keep the tourists safe but also to make sure they knew they were safe.

The squad room smelled of a dozen different cheap aftershaves and almost as many mouthwashes and would have made one sick if not used to it. And might make one sick even if they were used to it. The sweet smells were overwhelming and made it hard to breathe. The only smell worse was when someone loudly passed gas, either in response to something the lieutenant said or because he'd had too much fiber for breakfast.

The nonsmokers in the room were pleased with the smoking ban in all public buildings, enacted by Rudy Giuliani in 2003, because if cigarette smoke were added to the olfactory offenders it would be even worse. Musso wore Old Spice, and not one of the new designer fragrances for the younger generation. He wore the original scent his old man had worn when he was a kid. Five minutes into the meeting and he was already bored to tears. He was afraid he was becoming ADHD. He couldn't sit still. The ennui was excruciating. He was a street cop and couldn't bear paperwork or meetings.

Unlike in films and television police dramas there were no female detectives in the squadroom. There had been one, but shot in an ambush by homegrown terrorists, her wounds were not fatal but as yet she'd been unable to return to active duty. And even thought the other detectives had exacted their revenge by killing all of the terrorists, they were still pissed off that one of their own had been shot and would do everything in their power to keep it from ever happening again. The NYPD was a family and they would never allow a brother or sister to go unavenged.

"There are ladies...ahem... of the night, working in the daytime and approaching our fine gentlemen tourists and businessmen. I want youse to be on the lookout for them." Although a classically trained stage singer and actor, the lieutenant couldn't help falling into NYC colloquialisms. "Don't run them in. They're just trying to feed their kids, but let them know you're watching and er,...discourage them."

"I hope they approach me," said Det. "Big John" Sills, one of the oldest, along with Musso, and definitely the biggest detective in the room. At six-foot-five and somewhere north of three-hundred pounds, he intimidated perps with his size and his scowl. No lady of the night would dare to approach him. Scared to death that he would be that massive all over. He'd played on the offensive line in college and his natural athleticism enabled him to continue to pass the NYPD fitness tests in spite of his much heavier weight than the average law enforcement officer. What few outsiders knew was that Big was the sweetest man in the squad room and, although perfectly capable of going upside a perp's head if he needed to, it was the last thing he wanted to do. He loved God, his mother, his wife, his family, and his brothers and sisters in blue. And they were glad he was on their side.

Unwilling to hurt his feelings, none of the other detectives had asked Big exactly how much north of three-hundred he was. Indeed, he was a sensitive soul.

"Okay, gentlemen, not much is happening, but stay on your toes while you're out there—stay alert and maintain a high profile. The good citizens of New York need to know we're there for them and that we care about them. That's all."

"About damn time," Musso muttered under his breath. Then, "I'm gonna get a soda. You want one?"

"Hey, it wasn't that bad," said Maloney. "Less than thirty minutes. And no thanks, you know all I drink is wine, water and coffee."

"Yeah, but I'm getting older and I just don't have the patience for this shit anymore. So, you want a water? Coffee? It's too early for wine."

"No, I'm good. You don't have the patience for any shit anymore."

"I can still put up with your shit."

"Yeah, but that's because you love me."

The comment left Musso speechless but he managed to screw up his face at it.

***

Just before noon, Musso and Maloney collected their mufflers and overcoats from the coatrack in the squad room and bundled up to brave the weather en route to lunch. This time they decided on a Persian restaurant, one of Johnny's favorite lunch places, but he couldn't even get excited about his usual favorites—dolmeh, the falafal sandwich or the chicken barg—due to looking forward to snacking on MC's

Thanksgiving dinner after he got home from work.

As they studied menus, middle-eastern melodies most would think sounded like belly-dancing music provided an authentic backdrop. The air in the small restaurant was infused with the typical Persian spice aromas of clove, saffron and coriander. Deep shiny red paint and mirrors adorned most walls.

Unenthusiastically, Maloney ordered the dolmeh and chicken barg, just to see if he could force something down.

A few minutes later, a kindly server in traditional Persian garb of robe and headdress, brought their plates and even though it had been all of three minutes since they placed their orders, in the Middle-Eastern way, was softly and humbly apologetic for the delay. They remembered him from previous visits and Johnny thought he must be the owner.

As Musso plowed into a Koobideh sandwich, a mixture of ground beef and exotic spices, he noticed Maloney was only picking at his food.

"What's the matter, partner, upset stomach?"

"Nah, my heart's just not in it. I can't stop thinking about MC's stuffing and cranberries. I'm hoping she'll let me start on it when I get home tonight." Normally a healthy eater, he unenthusiastically pushed the food around on the plate.

"Well, just make sure you leave some for me for tomorrow," then rising, Musso added, " I'm going to the restroom."

After clearing the table next to where they sat a server dropped a tray full of dirty dishes. The incident, unwitnessed behind Musso's back, caused him to jump from his seat. "Damn, partner, why didn't you warn me? I'm not usually jumpy, but that shit was loud!"

He had to step around the server cleaning up the greasy mess before walking in the direction of the restroom.

The restaurant had small desserts and while Musso was in the restroom Maloney decided to see if he could eat one. As it turned out he tried two of the diminutive offerings: a key lime pie and a cannoli. Two led to a third when the s'mores looked good to him. When Musso returned he noticed the three small empty plates.

"Did you just have three desserts?"

"I usually have three. It's just that you're usually in the restroom when I do. Speaking of the restroom, have you had your prostate checked?"

'My prostate is fine."

"I'm just saying."

"What, what are you saying?"

"You aren't getting any younger. When you reach a certain age you should get that thing checked out. Geez, don't be so sensitive."

I'm not being sensitive, goddammit. Do you know anybody who's getting any younger?"

***

With the turkey and her stuffing in the oven, Mary Catherine decided she had time to get a manicure for the holiday season. It was a woman thing: a mani-pedi just made women feel better. Especially for the holidays. There was a shop across the street in the next block. She'd be gone less than an hour. She always figured the Vietnamese nail techs were talking about her in their native tongue, making jokes about her feet and toes, but she wouldn't dream of going to anyone else. As far as she was concerned, the Vietnamese manicurists were the best in the business.

Stepping onto the sidewalk, the first thing that assaulted her senses was the high-pitched scream of sirens, police and fire. She made the sign of the cross for whomever needed it and Johnny. She worried about him every time he left the house. If he only knew how much she worried he would have already finished law school and be making a career change.

***

Johnny entered the apartment and went straight to the kitchen.

As he peeked in the sizzling oven, Mary Catherine, in a replay of the morning, said, "Out—not until tomorrow. You may be the hotshot detective but I'm still the boss in the kitchen. Call Romanello's for a pizza and I'll join you in the living room in thirty minutes."

"Pizza? Sheesh. You're killing me here." Even if any other time he'd be thrilled with a Romanello's pie. He'd always believed that Chicago deep dish was overrated and New York-style pizza was the best and Romanello's made the best in the city.

"Yeah, I'm killing you. You know, your mother warned me about you before we got married. She told me you were a child when it came to your stomach."

"Well, I'm going to order a pie, eat it and then go to bed. At least I won't be able to think about turkey, stuffing and cranberries if I'm a sleep. And I'll close the bedroom door so I won't smell it. But with my luck I'll probably see visions of them dancing in my head."

Twenty minutes later the buzzer rang: the delivery from Romanello's. He had to be let in the building with a large everything pie, with anchovies.

"It's here," Johnny yelled to the closed kitchen door.

"Save me a slice. I'll be right there."

"You better hurry. I'm not happy with you right now and if you don't get in here it'll all be gone."

"And you won't get any stuffing tomorrow."

Johnny didn't like that. She had called his bluff and upped his ante and he'd folded. "Okay, fine. I'll have a slice waiting for you. And can you open a bottle of red and bring it with you?"

"Sure, hon. And you just think about how good dinner will be tomorrow and how much more you'll enjoy it with Carmine and Rosalie here."

Johnny's favorite Christmas movie, *Home Alone 2, Lost In New York* was on tv. The ironic thing about it was he always pulled for the bad guys, the housebreaking and burglar team of Joe Pesci and Daniel Stern. Christmas was his favorite time of year, and watching the movie, the night before Thanksgiving with the cold weather, and Christmas only a month away, he could let himself really get into the spirit.

Sitting there, with MC, bathed in the soft glow of the big screen television, and mellowed out with the help of the red wine, he could be satisfied with his life and just how content he was.

***

Waking early, MC turned on the oven and, after coating the sweet potato casserole in cinnamon and marshmallows, slid it into the heat. She repeated the process of sliding dishes into the oven with the homemade cranberry sauce and the broccoli rice casserole, but she'd have to wait until the sweet potatoes were perfect to put the pecan and apple pies in the oven.

An early riser for as long as he could remember—even when he was a kid—John took advantage of the holiday to sleep in. He got up in time to take a shower and have a quick breakfast—went into the kitchen, to the open shelf of cereal boxes and pulled down a huge box of Cap'n Crunch. He drowned the sugary cereal in a large bowl of skim milk; it wasn't sweet enough to suit him, so he added a rounded tablespoon-full of sugar over the cereal and poured a glass of orange juice—before the Macy's Parade started at nine. This was one of those days when he was happy he wasn't in uniform and didn't work in Manhattan. The guys in midtown were already busy as hell with a few million extra people in town.

Carefully balancing cereal and orange juice, Johnny walked to the living room, placed himself on the sofa, and set the big bowl and glass on the coffee table in front of him. Since dinner was all but ready, MC joined John so they could enjoy the parade together. She especially liked the show tunes performed from the year's most popular Broadway musicals at the terminus in front of Macy's. Still a big kid at heart, Johnny liked seeing Santa Claus bringing up the rear.

Carmine and Rosalie arrived at two, an hour before dinner, ample time for Rosalie and Mary Catherine to catch up over a glass of wine and John and Carmine to talk shop and watch football.

"Brr, it's cold," said Carmine, unwrapping the wool scarf from his neck. He'd lived in the city all his life but he still didn't handle the cold well.

"Aww, my big tough-guy police detective is cold," said Rosalie, feeling more sympathetic than she let on. She knew he had a difficult time staying warm and, in truth, it bothered her.

***

The Russians didn't celebrate Thanksgiving, a singularly American holiday. This caused tension between Arkady and Nora. Even though she hadn't been long in the U.S., she enjoyed celebrating its holidays and particularly loved the Christmas season, which she felt started with Thanksgiving.

At Arkady's apartment on the Upper East Side, Nora was trying to cook and watch the parade at the same time, while Arkady was doing what he does best, being an asshole. He truly loved her but he didn't share her excitement about the holidays or even understand it. Instead, he was concentrating on not getting sent back to Russia and having to give her up, by working his cellphone and putting together the next delivery of horse.

"Oh, listen…the cast from *The Phantom Of The Opera*. I love that music. Take me to see it. Pleeeze." Nora begged. "If you don't take me to see it you have to take me to Times Square for New Year's Eve," she whined.

"What's this phantom? Is that like a zombie?

"Oh, you," she said as she playfully slapped him on the shoulder. Nora at first accepted a date with Arkady because he had money to spend and she'd heard that he was a powerful man. But she had grown to care about him, to see past his rough exterior and hoped for something real and lasting. And if it were up to her, it would be.

***

Soft Christmas carols played from an iPod in a Bose SoundDock. The aroma of fresh-baked apple pie filled the apartment and added to the holiday comfort.

MC looked cute and preppie in jeans and a white Christmas sweater with an embroidered rendering of the Rockefeller Center Christmas tree.

Johnny's attire was less traditional. Watching the *Home Alone* movie the previous evening reminded him of his favorite holiday clothing. A red sweater reading, "Merry Christmas Ya Filthy Animals," the phrase McCauley Culkin uttered in the second *Home Alone* film to the Plaza Hotel staff as they ran from his room.

Rosalie hugged Mary Catherine warmly and handed her a bottle of 1998 Leoville Poyferre Bordeaux. A rich, luscious, amazingly complex red.

"Oh, you shouldn't have," said Mary Catherine. She hid away the bottle of pinot noir she had planned on opening.

"Nonsense! For such a lovely dinner, it deserves a special wine." It would have cost almost a week's salary for Carmine, had not a grateful citizen given it to him for rescuing his son from drugs. He shouldn't have accepted it. He knew he shouldn't. The department had rules against gifts, but he knew it was a superb wine and knew it would be perfect for Thanksgiving dinner and just couldn't refuse. His reasoning? He was sharing it with friends and he'd have only one glass, since wine—even good wine—made him sweat, it was okay.

John and Carmine moved to the living room and settled into the deep sofa in front of the large screen television. The Lions were kicking off to the Packers. Johnny hadn't liked the Packers since Brett Favre decamped for the Vikings and then ended up with his Jets. He'd thought then that Favre'd be his team's savior. The Jets head coach, Eric Mangini, apparently feeling the same way, had even named his newborn son Brett. It had not worked out for Gang Green, though. Neither John nor Carmine cared about either team, but it was football— on Thanksgiving—as American as apple pie.

John, being an amateur historian, was grateful for President Theodore Roosevelt, without whom the last Thursday in November would be a normal workday. Speaking softly but nonetheless carrying a big stick, the president had stepped in and saved football when Ivy League college presidents, which were the only schools that played the sport at the time, were thinking of calling a halt to football and outlawing games because of the injuries and even deaths. That would have meant the end of football. And then, he'd signed the bill establishing Thanksgiving. So, John knew that Americans owed the very existence of this great holiday to the nation's twenty-sixth president.

Early in the second quarter with the Pack leading, MC said, "Are you boys ready to eat?"

Hopping up, Johnny said, "Are you kidding? I've been ready for two days."

"Well," said MC, popping him on the butt like a football player would as he rushed by, "You finally get your wish."

Carmine rose and walked toward the dining room. "Football can wait," he said.

The table was beautifully set with fine china MC had inherited from her sainted grandmother and a mismatched array of various styles of red globe Christmas wine glasses she had discovered at various flea markets and antique stores and always pulled out for the holiday season.

The scene even moved the ever-tough, Carmine. "If it weren't filmed in black and white, this is the way the table in *It's A Wonderful Life* would look.

"Thank you, Carmine," MC said as she stood with her arm around Johnny's waist, getting slightly choked up and delighted that their friends were enjoying their holiday celebration.

Carmine and Johnny withdrew their wives' chairs and, as they sat,

Mary Catherine asked, "Rosalie, would you say grace?"

"Oh, I'd be honored."Gently grasping her silent pink glass-bead rosary in both hands and with her voice breaking slightly, she offered, "Heavenly Father, thank you for this wonderful food and wine you have provided." Johnny and Carmine both chuckled when the neighbor, Mr. Kensil's, miniature schnauzer, Killer, barked. "Thank you for allowing us to celebrate another Christmas season and the joyous occasion of Jesus's birth and Father would you please keep Carmine and Johnny safe as they go about their jobs of protecting the people of the great city of New York. Amen."

They all made the sign of the cross and repeated Amen. After giving Johnny a dirty look for laughing, Mary Catherine said, misty-eyed, "Thank you, Rosalie. That was just lovely."

She loved the holidays and could be overly emotional at this time of year.

Dinner passed quickly. MC and Johnny were brought up to date on Carmine and Rosalie's daughter, Anjelica, and Johnny and Carmine's job and holiday plans were discussed. After the Leoville Poyferre was emptied, MC retrieved a bottle of Rose' and they continued with dessert before retiring to the living room for coffee and more football.

"So, Rosalie, you want to hit the malls in New Jersey tomorrow?" Mary Catherine said over coffee. She was an admitted shopaholic and knew all the best malls. The Mall at Short Hills was her favorite but, on a NYC police detective's salary, she couldn't afford to shop there unless they were having serious sales, which they would on black Friday—the day after Thanksgiving.

"I'd love to, but I don't want to leave Carmine alone."

Carmine saw his chance and jumped in. "John, you want to watch football again tomorrow? There are a couple of college games on."

John, always taking advantage of an opportunity to bust Carmine's balls, gave him the business. "You sure you don't want to go shopping with the women tomorrow?"

Carmine didn't say a word. He flashed a look that could kill.

***

In John's car and after squaring the block once, Mary Catherine picked up Rosalie and the heater had it nice and toasty for her since she was chilled from standing on the sidewalk in front of their building.

MC turned on the wipers to try and brush off the light, dry snow flaking the windshield. All they did was make a horrible scraping sound against the frozen glass. She turned on the radio and changed it from the sports talk station Johnny'd been listening to the last time he was in the car to one playing Christmas music.

"Good morning," said Mary Catherine.

"Good morning, dear," said Rosalie, always cheerful, as usual. She removed her mittens and placed them in the top of her pocketbook on her lap.

"I'll have to remind Johnny to replace these wiper blades," she said.

"I bet he can get the mechanics in the department garage to do it."

"You're probably right," Mary Catherine said. "So, are you ready to fight the wars?" Black Friday at the malls in New Jersey was probably worse than any other place in the nation. The state was famous for its large number of malls and it was the only entire U.S. state to be designated urban by it's dense population.

"I'm always ready, MC."

"That's what I like to hear."

"How about a latte?" Mary Catherine asked. "My treat."

"That sounds lovely."

Their first stop on their route was a service plaza, where MC pulled up to a Starbuck's drive thru, with easy access, sited as it was between the north and south lanes of the turnpike. The smell of aromatic coffee came through the order window to fill the car. Mary Catherine ordered a grande' skinny Cinnamon Dolce latte and Rosalie, an eggnog latte. The flavors perfect for the holiday season. As MC pulled away from the drive thru and with her window still lowered from placing her order, she heard a young man in his twenties walking across the parking lot, yell in her direction, "Go Jets." She knew he'd seen the bumper sticker Johnny'd put on the front end. And her husband wouldn't be happy to learn it brought her unwanted attention from young men. Underway again, it took longer than usual, due to shoppers' traffic, to get to the Short Hills Mall. Although New Jersey traffic was always bad, Black Friday amped it to extreme. It took well over an hour to reach the exclusive mall. Pulling into the massive, and full, parking lot, Mary Catherine said, "I hope you don't mind If we go to Sephora. I need some perfumes."

"Of course not, MC. Anywhere is fine. This is a treat for me. Carmine wouldn't do this for love nor money." Rosalie intended to enjoy herself.

"Johnny's the same way. But, this way, we get a girls' day out."

"Amen." Rosalie was almost giddy.

They found a remote parking space, walked for five minutes and finally reached a mall entrance. Inside, they checked a mall directory for Sephora, passed a Coach Store and MC mentioned that Johnny needed a new wallet to replace the worn out, scarred leather one he'd had since they married.

Entering, Rosalie said, "Carmine needs a new billfold too. His old one is so tired."

Once inside, Mary Catherine bought a purse for her niece and Rosalie decided she could use a new pocketbook, also. They thanked Heaven for the sales.

The cute young Asian woman that waited on them at the Coach store wore a stylishly short hairdo, dyed blonde with a raspberry streak.

Happy with their purchases, and leaving the store loaded down with bags and smiles on their faces, they braved the crowds of the broad hallways. In minutes they were hot, dressed as they were for the outdoor temperatures.

***

Down a long narrow hallway, dimly lit due to a pair of burned out light bulbs, the apartment was on the rear of the building, its view overlooking the Hudson River and the ships and yachts streaming to and from upriver ports, the cargo ships on a mission, the yachts more leisurely. U.S. rivers were still an important part of the nation's transport economy, and the Hudson was one of the most important for the delivery of goods both of the legal and illegal variety.

The buzzer announced Carmine's arrival. He'd placed his laminated NYPD parking placard in the car's dash, and parked by the fire hydrant in front of the building. He'd move it if he heard sirens.

One o'clock and Johnny turned on his new widescreen television to the first game of the day. Ohio State's Buckeyes were kicking off to the Spartans of Michigan State. John wore a green NY Jets sweatshirt. Carmine, a blue and red Giants hoodie and his only pair of dungarees. Older than his age, he thought denim was just for kids. Even on a holiday weekend, both were armed, John wearing a Glock Model 19 9mm, Carmine preferring the more traditional Smith & Wesson 5946, also in 9mm, both modified to the NYPD standard of a twelve-pound pull. They both loaded new rounds in a magazine they rotated out once a month just to be sure the spring-loaded clip would function like it should even if it might be considered an unnecessary inconvenience by others. John, who smoked only on special occasions and felt like the holiday season qualified, offered Carmine a cigar, then opened windows in the living room and kitchen to get a draft passing through the apartment in an attempt to clear out the stogie smell. Because of MC's scented candles the apartment smelled pleasing, unlike most Bronx apartments which smelled like old people. Indeed, many Bronx residents were senior citizens and had lived there a lifetime. Johnny complained good-naturedly about the candles saying they made him sneeze but even he had to admit they were better than the uncloaked smell of the decades-old apartment. And he liked to joke that, besides, the smell of old people made him sneeze, too.

Carmine walked over to the half-open sliding glass door to the balcony, looked through the rain dappled glass toward the river, and said, "That's a nice view John, a real nice view."

Johnny asked him, "Did you have any breakfast, partner?

"Yeah, I had an omelette in the diner across from my building. Speaking of breakfast, what's that stuff they eat for breakfast in the south?"

"Oatmeal…Cream of Wheat?"

No, man. No…Oh yeah, grits."

"What's a grit?"

"Not a grit, grits.

"If you say so. Damn, it's cold with that door open, but MC will have my ass if she smells these cigars. She even hates it when I smoke one on the balcony." The sounds of traffic and sirens on the streets below was also louder with the door open. Sirens were a constant, twenty-four hours a day in New York. Like a lot of New Yorkers did to their furniture, the gold, crushed velvet sofa on which they sat and coordinating green-and-gold plaid chairs had been slip-covered in clear vinyl to protect them from odors and spills. A colorful painting in a gilded frame of the Ferris wheel at Coney Island hung above the couch. Johnny and Mary Catherine had ridden it on their first time to go out.

She still wouldn't let him forget it, and always told people that he took her to Nathan's on Coney Island for hotdogs instead of a nice dinner on their first date. The couch was draped in the Jets blanket that MC let John pull out only when he was watching football. A six-foot wide by three-foot deep 'balcony' off the living room would barely hold two people, but that's what one got for the money in the South Bronx. Three flowerpots adorned it, each with purple cabbages arranged around dwarf blue spruces. Crystalline raindrops sparkled where they lighted on the the deep green edged purple leaves the night before. Mary Catherine had chosen the plants for their ability to flourish during winter and indeed they thrived in the early season cold.

John got up and went to the kitchen, stepping, not for the first time, on a creaky floorboard. "Damn, I need to get somebody to fix that. MC has been on my ass about it for weeks." Truth was after almost ten years living there, John had grown accustomed to the sounds of the old apartment—the creaks of the floorboards, the pops behind the walls and the groaning pipes. The sounds that made it feel like home. As he opened the refrigerator, "You want a beer Carmine—an Other Half?" The Other Half, a Bronx brewery, was one of New York's top-rated beer-makers.

"Well, damn, man, take care of the little lady. Call somebody, then. You owe it to her the way she puts up with your ass. No thanks. You got a diet Pepsi?"

"What do you think? Want a little hit of bourbon in it? Got Blanton's."

"No, partner, just plain old diet Pepsi. Sheesh."

"How about a Yoo-hoo, then? That'd be better than Pepsi for Thanksgiving."

"Listen to me. A. Diet. Pepsi. Period."

"Okay, okay. It's the holidays. Just thought you might want to live a little."

"I am living. I'm smoking a cigar and not working, *And* watching football. That's celebration enough for me, as long as I get a damn diet Pepsi. I swear to God. You could outdrink my parish priest and he's a goddamn Irishman. Course you are, too."

John set their drinks on the glass-topped wood coffee table and said, "Cool. I won't ask again. And I'll take that as a compliment. I hear your priest is a helluva drinker. You ought to ask him to hang out with us sometime...I wonder how the chicks are doing." When he leaned back on the sofa, hands behind his head, the Jets blanket slipped from where it rested on the back to the cushions. He refolded it so the big green and white Jets logo showed and put it back in place. MC had worked hard to make the apartment suitable for a man, a NYC police detective, no less, and also give it a look that a girly-girl like herself could live in. For the most part she'd accomplished it, except for days like this when he messed it up with the blanket.

"The girls are fine, John. They're shopping. Mary Catherine has your credit card. She's happy as shit. And as long as you're careful not to piss me off I won't tell them you called them chicks. And Father Ryan shows up at the K of C, sometimes. We could meet him there. The guys that hang out there can really party. Whole bunch of Irishmen drinking God's whiskey and playing poker. But you don't want to play with them...a couple of them hold a rosary in the hand that ain't holding the cards. Think that gives them an advantage. Shit, saying the rosary while playing poker...like God cares if they win or lose."

"The women do the same thing playing bingo."

"Yeah, but it ain't the same. It's worse playing poker. Jesus didn't like gambling, you know."

"Well, then they shouldn't play poker at all." In John's mind the matter was settled.

Musso had been less devout as a young man, but now, in his advancing years, he not only went to mass on Easter Sunday and Christmas, but attended regularly, went to Reconciliation once a month and hung out at the Knights of Columbus Hall, figuring that fellowship with other Catholics couldn't hurt, especially since his job required that he hang out with the worst kind of the city's criminal element. But he had to admit that he liked Mass better when he was a kid, when it was said in Latin rather than English. He liked the history, ritual and symbolism of the original Romance language.

Michigan State intercepted a pass returning it for a touchdown and the green-and-white-clad cheerleaders somersaulted on the sideline.

Carmine cursed loudly, at the interception.

John said, "Damn, partner, use your inside voice. Besides, I thought you didn't care who won."

Musso said, "I'm Italian. This *is* my inside voice. And I *don't* care who wins. I just can't stand stupid mistakes, and that dumbass qb should've never thrown the ball. Should've taken a sack." Maloney agreed with him but he'd never admit it to Carmine.

The talk eventually got around to the job. Johnny first: "By the way, you've been talking more about retirement lately. How much longer you think you're gonna give it?"

"I don't know. I'm thinking five more at the most."

"Cool. I probably won't even last that long. I hope to be practicing in no more than two or three. What're you gonna do?"

"I'm thinking me and Rosalie will move to Miami. Get out of the cold. I've socked away some cash. Buy a nice boat. Live the life. You know, when you're down there you can smell the ocean every way you turn—saltwater, clean fresh air. That's the way to live. It's healthier than New York. Still, charter boats are pretty expensive. I'll probably need a partner—an investor—but nevertheless, buy a boat; I'll captain it and just do some fishin'. You know there are more former New Yorkers in Miami now than native Floridians." He didn't know if that was true or not, but there were a helluva lot of former New Yorkers living in Miami. "I figure they'd be willing to pay somebody to take 'em fishin'. Especially a retired New York City Police detective. And the Jets come to town once a season, so I can see some New York football even if it is the effin' Jets."

That struck a nerve with Maloney: "Better than your goddamn Giants. In fact me and MC would probably come down if you got tickets for a Jets game.

"Watch it," said Musso.

"So—you, fishing?"

"I shit you not."

"Sounds good, but do you know how to fish?"

"I can learn. How hard can it be? Bait your hook. Throw it in the water. Pull out the fish."

"Okay, cool. At least MC and I will have a free place to stay when we come down."

"That you will, partner. Any time you want."

"So, what do you think the kids are doing?"

"Hernandez and Louis?"

"What other kids you think I'd be talking about?"

"Shit. I don't know. I hope they're workin' the fuckin' Zombies. Newbies always work holiday weekends. God bless 'em. And it helps protect their cover. Bad guys would never think we'd have people undercover on a holiday weekend."

"If they didn't, we'd have to. Cheers," John tilted his bottle of beer at his partner.

"Cheers." Carmine leaned over and plunked his plastic bottle of Diet Pepsi against Johnny's bottle of Other Half.

***

Morris "Mo" Louis and Antonio "Jun" Hernandez were walking toward Valentine. Louis wore a Knicks cap, blue and orange. Hernandez wore a Yankees promotional cap from St. Patrick's Day; so instead of the white NY logo residing on Yankee blue, it rested on kelly green. Drinking crap coffee they picked up at the walk-up window of a bodega. But at least it was hot and smelled better than it tasted. Almost time for them to split up.

Morris said, "Man, this sucks—working Thanksgiving weekend."

"Hernandez drew his index finger back and forth across his thumb and said, "This is the world's smallest violin playing '*My Heart Bleeds For You.*'"

"Louis said, "That would be funny if it were funny."

Ignoring the comment, "You wanted to be a cop. At least you don't have a girlfriend. Anne isn't happy with me for missing Thanksgiving with her and her family. Besides, next year somebody else will have to work it. We won't be the newbies anymore."

"That doesn't help me now."

"Okay, this is where we go our separate ways. Can't let any Zombies see us together."

"I don't want any Zombies to see me at all," Louis said. "They're ugly undead people walking around. They scare me."

"Mo, you're a funny dude." That comment reminded Hernandez of how Louis used his humor to keep all the trainees loose when things got too intense at the academy. Otherwise the tension would have gotten to all of them. Every class at the academy worried that somebody, giving in to the pressure, would eat his gun.

***

Rev was chilling on the Black Friday. Enjoying the afternoon with one of his ladies and a glass of his favorite cognac while watching college football. He still was of a mind he could have played with those guys. But his mind was also on business. He was almost ready to implement his audacious plan. After the holiday weekend. He'd kept it from his inner circle, although something told him Darelle was beginning to have suspicions. His man couldn't possibly know what, because Rev hadn't even voiced the plan aloud, but he felt like Darelle suspected something.

He couldn't remember the girl's name but she got up to go to the bathroom. He popped her on the butt as she walked by and then, even though he was on the phone, he spoke in her direction. "Hey babe, pour me another two fingers of the De Montesquiou while you're up? Before you get tied up in the bathroom?" The upward inflection at the end made it sound like a request, like he was asking. Both knew he was not.

She nodded—but it appeared that it was somewhat grudgingly. Bad mistake on her part if it was. Rev was pretty easygoing but he wasn't used to people disrespecting him and he wouldn't tolerate it in his own home. His wealth and status had earned him the respect of others. And his carriage and demeanor demanded it. A call from Marquise beeped in.

"I've got to take this," Rev said to the other caller.

"Yeah, Marquise. How's the holiday business?—That's not too bad. Just make sure they work a little later tonight. We can probably make it up."

His VP of Operations had told him even before getting the numbers that sales would probably be down five, maybe ten per cent from a typical Friday. But since they'd anticipated it they were prepared for it. They'd get most of it back with a few extra hours.

***

Rosalie and Mary Catherine decided on a late lunch at The Cheesecake Factory to fortify themselves for more shopping. Give them strength because shopping was such hard work, especially on Black Friday.

The high ceiling, about thirty feet to the rafters, and the faux painting was the same as in Cheesecake Factories in malls throughout the country. Rosalie chose the Factory nachos and a glass of sweet Reisling. Mary Catherine opted for the Grilled Chicken Tostada Salad and a glass of white Sangria.

The older woman giggled, covering her mouth with her hand. "I feel so naughty. I shouldn't be drinking wine in the daytime."

Mary Catherine agreed. "I shouldn't either but it's a special occasion."

"What do you think the boys are doing?" Rosalie asked.

"Probably watching football, and if I know Johnny—and I do—having a glass of red wine. I just hope for his sake he's not smoking a cigar. I'll ring his little Irish neck if he smells up my house."

Chapter Nine
Deep Undercover

Thanksgiving over, Maloney and Musso called in their CI, Lamar.

"So, you've put the word out on the street we want somebody in the Zombies?" Maloney asked Lamar.

"Yeah, man. I found just the right dude."

"Talk to us," said Musso.

"Yeah, I never seen him around before, but I hear he's connected."

"Well, if you're gonna vouch for him, he better be," said Maloney.

"When you want him here?"

"When can he be here?" asked Maloney.

"I'll have to ask my man knows where he stays."

"Ask him. The sooner the better," Carmine suggested.

"Cool, but now I gotta depart," said Lamar.

"Okay, but don't disappear on us," said Maloney, "or we'll punch your ticket."

"I hear you. I'm gonna hook you up."

"See that you do," said Musso.

"Come on, dude, have faith in a brother."

Lamar left the precinct and walked to the offsite-betting office just a few blocks west of Fort Apache. His buddy Melvin was a regular customer and hung out there a lot even when he wasn't flush and didn't have the cash for placing wagers.

To the Pakistani man working in the cage he fist-bumped him under the bars, and, too loudly for the small room, said, "Yo, my brother, you seen my man Melvin this morning?"

In the quiet, polite voice of a soft spoken middle-eastern immigrant he replied, "No, my friend, he doesn't usually make it in on Mondays. Slow day at the track, you know. Probably tomorrow."

"Thanks bro, I'll be back." Lamar's personality was larger than life and took up as much space in the small room as his body.

Entering the betting office the next day, Lamar saw his bro, Melvin.

"My man, sup?" said Lamar.

"Ah, you know, same ole shit," Melvin seemed despondent.

"Yeah, I hear you, but I need some help. What about the dude knows the Zombies?"

"Yeah, my man, DeAngelo."

"That's the brother's name?"

"Yeah man, that's the dude—De."

 "You need to hook a brother up. I need to talk to him."

"No prob, bro. Be here same time tomorrow, and I'll make sure the brother be here.

"Done and done," said Lamar and he fist bumped Melvin.

Lamar spent the rest of the day scouting buildings that looked like they'd be easy to enter. He spotted a couple of possibilities and made a mental note to make a return visit to them after hours on some night soon.

***

Arriving early, Lamar wanted to make sure he didn't miss DeAngelo. He didn't know what the dude looked like, but he hoped Melvin had described him to DeAngelo.

He'd been there an hour before a tall, athletic brother slumped in wearing a Knicks jersey, new dark-blue dungarees and old school, black, high-top Converse All-Stars. A nascent Afro made him look even taller. He sported nervous eyes that danced sneakily from side-to-side, as if their dance would keep anyone from noticing him.

Dude looked his way, recognition flashing instantaneously in the intelligent eyes. Obviously DeAngelo. Walking over to where Lamar leaned against a table used for filling out racing forms, bro extended a long arm to fist-bump. Looked like he could have reached him from across the room.

"My man," Lamar said more quietly than usual, picking up on the tall man's wish to be discreet.

"Sup." More of a greeting than a question. One could tell he didn't care.

"So, you know the Zombies?"

"Yeah, bro," he responded, chill, still glancing about furtively. "I know the dudes."

"And you willing to help the man?"

"Yeah, bro."

"An interrogative—why?

"I don't have a degree in marketing. Can't get a good job. I need the bread, man. I gots to eat."

"I hear you. Times is tough."

"Amen to that."

"The 5-0 you need to see is Detectives Maloney and Musso. Musso's a hardass but Maloney's a good dude, even if he be's a little square." He used the street term 5-0 for police, popularized by Jack Lord in the Hawaii Five-O television show of the 70's, even if he was too young to have watched it. It was now a part of the lexicon of the street and always would be. "They be expecting you, so get yo ass on over to Fort Apache real quick-like. Know where it is?"

"You shittin' me? Evabody know Fort Apache."

"Aiiight then. Git yo self on over there." He didn't mean for that to sound as insulting as it did, but it was too late to worry about it now.

DeAngelo started the short walk toward Fort Apache. In the meantime Lamar left a voice mail on Detective Maloney's cell phone letting him know who to expect.

The new confidential informant pulled the oversized brass handle to open one of the famous precinct's noisy doors. He approached Sergeant Cabrera's large aerie, from which the man surveyed everything and everyone below the elevated perch.

"What can I do you for?" the sergeant asked.

"I need to see detectives Maloney or Musso."

"Who's asking?"

"DeAngelo."

"DeAngelo who?"

"Just DeAngelo. They be expecting me."

"I guess we'll find out, won't we, just DeAngelo." Cabrera picked up the phone and called upstairs to the detectives' squad room.

"Yeah, detective, I have a...er, *gentleman* here to see youse, says you and detective Musso are expecting him...He says it's DeAngelo— just DeAngelo."

Sergeant Cabrera watched DeAngelo studying the photos and thought it curious that a street dweller would show so much interest in the pictures of NYPD police commissioners.

DeAngelo considered the large framed photos of the NYPD's lineage of their highest ranking officers hanging on the wall pretending not to listen to the one-sided conversation. He was genuinely interested in the picture of Teddy Roosevelt prior to his unsuccessful run for Mayor of New York City, before being elected governor of New York and ultimately becoming the 26th President of the United States after William McKinley died in office and the roughrider, being vice president, succeeded him.

Maloney had already heard Lamar's message so, unsurprised by DeAngelo's arrival, Maloney told the Desk Sergeant they would be right down.

"Uh, sir," he said to the back of DeAngelo's Afro-covered head, "the detectives will be with you right away."

"Cool." DeAngelo appeared unaffected by being in Fort Apache. Anyone watching wouldn't know if it was because he'd been there before, and had nothing to fear, or was just too cool to be bothered. An astute observer probably would have guessed the latter.

It took ten minutes for the detectives to appear. They delayed on purpose, hoping to throw DeAngelo off his game, to let him know— make sure he knew—that they were in control from the start. They eschewed taking the slow-moving elevator from the second floor, instead descending the broad staircase.

However, betraying his excitement, Maloney practically leapt from the last step of the wide stairwell to the slick tile floor. He'd been the more excited one about this opportunity anyway. Musso was more laid back, glancing around furtively as if he weren't sure why he was there.

Maloney extended a hand. "Detective Maloney—nice to meet you."

"DeAngelo." Low and quiet, his voice could only be described as surly. He wore his surliness like a badge of honor, as if he were pissed off at being alive and there was nothing he could do about it except to get even with life by kicking the world's ass.

"Musso." Showing that he could be equally surly.

Maloney turned to his left and said, "Let's go in here." Before DeAngelo could enter the main corridor, he had to pass through an x-ray machine, much like those in airports, to show that he wasn't packing. A blond wood door off the hallway opened to a small conference room, with a scarred wood laminate table that seated six people comfortably. Wheeled armchairs were dressed in faded beige fabric stained from too many coffee spills and too many cigarette burns inflicted before the smoking ban in government buildings. The walls and ceiling saddened by nicotine stains from decades of the same cigarettes. Harsh neon lights lighted the otherwise dreary room.

As senior detective, Musso started, "What can you do for us?" That's all that mattered to him—how the snitch could help them.

"Whatchu want?"

Musso said, "Anything you can get us on the Zombies. Anything and everything."

"How much does this gig pay?"

Maloney, sensing that his partner and DeAngelo were already having problems, jumped in. "It depends on how you produce."

"What if I be producing?"

"DeAngelo, the answer is it depends—it depends on the perceived value of the information. We have a fund for paying CIs, based on the department's years of experience. It isn't up to Detective Musso and me. It's based on the NYPD's history with CIs and how much the higher-ups think a piece of information is worth."

DeAngelo rubbed his head then drew his palm down his face, stretching his nose out of shape. "Shit. I gonna trust some pig pulling down six figures to take care of me?"

Musso hadn't heard anyone refer to a policeman as a pig in years and actually thought it was hilarious. He had to try hard not to laugh out loud. That would really get in the way of he and DeAngelo getting along.

"I don't know what to tell you, DeAngelo. Except ask your bro's buddy, Lamar. He's been a CI for a while and I think he's pretty happy with the deal."

"Cool. I'll be in touch," he said.

"Don't get lost," said Musso.

"I know where y'all at."

"Use a map if you forget." Musso just didn't like the man. Of course there weren't many snitches he did like. Maloney hoped that that wouldn't come back to bite them and cause the man not to want to work with them.

"What's your problem with him?" Maloney asked his partner.

"I don't know. He's likeable, I just don't like him. I can sense that he practices being likeable."

Chapter Ten
Strategy

Detective Louis approached the dealer he'd made contact with a couple of days previously.

"So," the dealer said to Louis, "You want a job or you jus' wanna hang out on the street?"

"Si, dude. I want a job. You hiring?" Louis' attempt at Spanish was laughable. Jun had been teaching him some basic Spanish since much of Tagalog, the main Filipino language was heavily influenced by it.

"Don't do the hirin,' but I can hook you up with the dude that do."

"Righteous. I'll be back. Make it happen. Mañana," and Detective Louis fist-bumped him before making his exit. He really needed to work on his street talk, his mix of bro street and unaccented Spanish was cartoonish at best.

Louis texted Hernandez. Told him he'd scored and was heading back to the barn.

Back at Fort Apache, Louis saw Musso and Maloney in a hallway and, proud of himself, wanted to tell them about it immediately.

"Detectives, a street corner dude is giving me an intro to the man that does the hiring."

"That's real cool, Louis," said Maloney, meaning it. The kids reminded him of himself not that long ago, when he was trying to make his bones on the job and would take any crap assignment offered him to move up.

"Yeah, good job," said the unenthusiastic Musso, "How's Hernandez doing?"

"I don't think he's in place yet, but he'll be back soon and we can find out then."

Hernandez returned to Fort Apache shortly after five o'clock.

"Not yet man, but I'm close," was his answer to Louis' query.

"Go tell the seniors then, 'cause I'm making you look bad."

"Thanks, partner. I'll return the favor. You can count on it."

"Yeah, sure you will. You said that when we were running sprints at the academy. Didn't happen then. Ain't gonna happen now."

Hernandez told Maloney and Musso that he thought he'd be in with the Zombies by the next day, the end of the week at the latest.

Said Musso, "Get on the ball, kid. Daylight's burnin'. We can't get it back."

"Will do, detective,"

***

Arkady was pissed off and it showed on his furrowed brow and in the way he clenched his fists, cracking his knuckles loudly. He wanted more business in the Bronx and wasn't making much headway. They were doing well in Queens and Brooklyn and even Manhattan, but the Bronx was the apple of the NYC drug trade and unless he was able to increase their foothold his days in the US and his nights with the beautiful Nora would be numbered.

And he couldn't have that. He'd grown accustomed to the warm nights with the spicy Colombian.

***

It was two days before the street dealer arranged for Marquise to show up to meet Detective Louis who by this time had decided Mo, short for his given name, Morris, would be a good street name. Gesturing to the undercover detective, the dealer said to Marquise, "This is the dude I was telling you about."

Detective Louis said, "Mo, sup?"

Marquise looked over the much smaller man skeptically and nodded.

"So, you want to be a Zombie?"

"Affirmative."

"Why?"

"Ah, you know, earn some bread. I like being outdoors. Talk to chicks. Get some sunshine and fresh air."

Marquise didn't know what to make of the brother. "At least you're honest."

"That I am...and a hard worker. You could do a helluva lot worse than me."

"The only concern I got is your talking to the chicks. In the Zombies we're all about the 'mob'—Money over bitches. Remember that."

That was the only red flag for Marquise, but it was a minor one and wouldn't keep him from bringing him on board. The kid had personality. Rev might have sensed something else, but the kid'd never meet Rev. The Zombies organization was set up so that lower level street dealers would never meet "The Man."

***

Maloney beat Musso into the office the next morning.

"Dude, we've got to get the new snitch working. I'm going to call the number he gave us."

Musso said, "Fine, but I've told you before: do not call me 'dude'. I'm too old for that kid shit."

"Okay, okay, but one question—did you put on your scratchy underwear by mistake this morning? 'S' that what's making you so cranky?"

"Now, I have a question for you. How long we been partners? I'm always cranky. You should know that by now."

"I know, I know. I do. Too many years, but you seem even crankier than usual."

"Maybe I wouldn't be so cranky if you didn't call me dude."

Ignoring that comment with a dismissive shrug and a tilt of his head, Maloney pulled out his latest generation yuppie iPhone and dialed the number.

He heard a short ring through the fancy phone before it connected. "De."

Maloney said, "DeAngelo?"

"This is De. Sup?"

"Yeah, De, this is Detective Maloney speaking."

"Sup?" he said again.

"DeAngelo, I'm here with Detective Musso and we'd like you to come in for a little strategizing. When could you be here?"

"I might have some time late this afternoon before I go out to meet the ladies. I'd have to be done in time for happy hour, you know. Two-for-one drinks for the females. That way the alcohol does most of my work for me."

"All right then, four o'clock, here at the precinct?"

"Ten-four. Hey, I'm just fuckin' with you. Always wanted to say that to a cop.

"Well, you said it. See you at four."

"And I was jus' makin' that shit up about happy hour. I don't go to no yuppie fern bars." DeAngelo laughed before he clicked off.

"I hope this guy can deliver," Maloney said to his partner. He'd wanted this for a long time and he hoped it would pay off in a big way.

***

It seemed to DeAngelo that the pigs were eager, which would be good for him. Yeah, this was going to be easier than he'd expected. He could play them right into his hands.

DeAngelo wore a purple dashiki and sunglasses. The shades looked like Oakleys but might have been knockoffs. Impossible to tell. One could buy perfect copies of almost anything on NYC streets. Fake Rolexes, Louis Vuitton handbags, Oakleys, cubic zirconias that to the less sophisticated eye could pass for Harry Winstons. He entered the massive wood doors of Fort Apache. This time detectives Musso and Maloney were downstairs waiting for him.

DeAngelo grinned, smarter than your average street thug and more aware than most, he knew he had them in the palm of his hand.

Although Musso's was less enthusiastic than Maloney's, both detectives glad-handed him. Maloney led them into the same conference room they had commandeered previously. They sat in the same chairs as before.

Maloney said, "De, welcome, how you doin?"

"Aiight."

"So, we want to get this ball rollin,'" said Musso.

"Aiight."

Musso again, "Can you say anything besides aiight".

DeAngelo shrugged. Then he leaned back in the chair, his hands with his long fingers interlaced behind his head. He hadn't removed his shades.

To his partner, Musso said, "Detective Maloney, I think we've made a mistake."

Maloney said, "Let's just relax and start over," Maloney countered. "De, what do you think your approach should be?"

"My approach?" He leaned forward and clasped his long fingers in front of him on the table. "I think my goddamn approach should be to focus some of my efforts on the goddamn Russians. Word on the street is they've got something big up their sleeves planned for the Zombies."

"Damn. Those Russians are nothing but a bunch of assholes.

They'd fight each other just as soon as battle the Zombies," Musso said.

This wasn't exactly what they'd expected. But recalling the shootout at the yacht club that left three middle-aged white men dead, Maloney flicked a sideways glance at his partner and kept silent to keep DeAngelo talking. They'd thought at the time it probably had something to do with the Russians and the Zombies. Maloney turned to De and eased out a few painful words. "Can you elaborate?"

"Elaborate? Aiight. Like I said, word is on the street those old white bastards tried to rip off the Zombies. Zombies wasn't soft, though, and they left three of them old dudes deader'n shit, 'n now the rest of 'em want revenge. Those Russians, they all be OG's—old gangsters—you know. They be bad but they don't think. They ain't smart like the brothers."

"The Russians aren't exactly our target here," Musso said, "but we'll take it."

"Word is the Russians want to take over the Bronx…and I thought, you know…the devil you know." Musso nodded, thinking for a brief moment that DeAngelo was a helluva lot smarter than he looked.

Maloney said, "Yeah, we hear you. We'll take it."

Then DeAngelo continued: "Besides, those damn Russkies are into a lot more shit than jus' drugs. Contract killing, child porn, sex trafficking. Like I said, at least with the Zombies you know whatchu got."

Feeling like he was dragging it out of him, Musso said, "So what's the word on the street about the Zombies?"

DeAngelo said, straight-faced, "They not on the street. They be dead." Then breaking up with a huge laugh, said, "Get it? They be Zombies. They ain't alive, they be dead. Gotcha with that one, didn't I?"

Intervening between the two before it escalated, Maloney said, "Yeah you got us, but what's up with them?"

"I hear they be expanding their territory, moving east toward Co-op City," referring to the massive complex in the East Bronx, the largest cooperative housing development in the world, that, if it were an actual municipality, would be the tenth largest city in the state of New York.

"Shit," Musso said, "And we've been able to keep CC relatively clean."

"Relatively is relative," said DeAngelo with a smartass grin. His intelligent wit belied his street appearance.

Musso was on his feet: "How much more of his bullshit do I have to put up with?"

Maloney quickly intervened, placing his hands on his partner's shoulders with enough pressure to keep him from DeAngelo: "Just relax, Rock. I have a feeling about this. I think it's going to pay off. Let's give him a chance."

"Fine, but I'm keeping him on a short leash."

DeAngelo eyed the detectives with searing contempt. "So now I'm your goddamn dog?"

"Now, you calm down, De. Nobody's calling you a dog," Maloney said, as he blazed Musso with a look that could ignite coal.

"Check out the goddamn Russians," DeAngelo said, "Peace. Out," then he tapped his chest twice with his open right hand, kissed his index and middle finger, pointed them skyward and hastily took his exit.

Musso collapsed back into the chair and let out a deep sigh. "There's just something about him I really don't like. I don't trust him. There's something strange."

"You mean stranger than the usual street-person who lives under bridges, eats out of dumpsters and barely survives?"

Musso held up his hands palms out in a gesture of placation. "Okay, okay, but still..."

Maloney was emphatic, but also pissed off at Musso's lack of tact in dealing with DeAngelo. "Just give him a few days. I think it'll be worth it. But, hey, you played bad-cop real well. You're getting better at it."

"Who says I was playing?"

"Yeah, right. You're not that good of an actor, but you even had me going there for a minute. I wasn't sure."

And you were a real good good-cop.

Thanks, but next time let's change roles.

"Nah. You don't have the chops for it. And besides you look too much like a choir boy to play bad-cop since you shaved off that 'stache."

"Yeah, well, you'll see."

***

The first weekend in December and Johnny decided to surprise MC with tickets to the *Radio City Music Hall Christmas Spectacular.*

He got home from work and found his wife in the kitchen cooking dinner. He stole up behind her and, as he put his arms around her waist, kissed her on the neck. "What are you doing Saturday night, babe?" he asked.

Spinning in his arms then pushing him away, she said, "Stop that. That tickles. What? This Saturday night? What are you talking about?"

He pulled a pair off tickets from his jacket pocket. "I'm going to the Radio City Christmas Spectacular. If you're sweet, you can be my date."

Mary Catherine squealed with delight, then, after thinking about it a moment, said, "Johnny, we haven't seen that show since the first Christmas we were dating."

"I remember. Why do you think I got 'em?"

"You're so romantic."

"That's not what you usually say."

"But I give you credit when you deserve it."

"That you do. So, that means you'll go?"

"You just try and go without me, buster." She playfully punched him in the ribs.

***

Arkady had called a meeting of his lieutenants to outline his plan for a strike on the Zombies. He made sure everyone understood the importance of avenging the deaths of their fallen comrades. In truth, he had no feelings for those casualties except for the way it reflected on his reputation. He would not be thought of as weak.

"I'm getting pissed and you won't like me pissed." Arkady liked American television and adopted a modified version of the line the Hulk used in the old television show he'd seen in reruns. His minions needed little convincing. They also knew their job was to hail Caesar, praising Arkady's brilliance and ingenuity even if they thought the idea was crap. Thus when he outlined a bold plan to attack where they would least expect—on their home turf at the Valentine Street headquarters—at a time they wouldn't expect when there would be fewer Zombies around, Arkady asked, "So what do you assholes think?"

Choruses of: "Brilliant... Genius...The greatest battle plan of all time."

His ego fed, Arkady could now make it happen. He admired and was more like Napoleon than he would ever want to admit. He pretended he didn't care what others thought, when in truth he would be paralyzed without the approval of his underlings, even though he shouldn't have concerned himself with their opinions. Like some in history, who, if they'd followed their own counsel, might have been better off.

***

Detective Louis was assigned to work with another dealer, the duration of which would be determined by Marquise. Louis knew the dealer was checking him out, but it was also beneficial for the detective, as he could observe, listen, make mental notes and find out all he could.

"Dude, so how you like this gig?" Louis asked.

"Ah, you know. 'S a job," the dealer said, "but difference is, with most jobs you don't have to worry 'bout goin' to jail or gettin' shot."

"Yeah, that kind of sucks, don't it?"

The dealer was street smart, but very street. Louis was surprised that he could count the cash. He tried to be obtuse, but he hoped the dude would give him something.

"What should I expect with the Zombies? Promotions, expanded territory, what?"

"I don't know man. I'm a nobody."

"Ain't no thing, just wondering what I'm gettin' into." Louis backed off. Didn't want to push him too hard—cause him to ask questions. After being closed-mouth most of the morning the dealer finally threw him a bone. "I'm a peon. They don't tell me nothing, but, I keep my ears open. That's what a smart man do. And I'll tell ya. There's something big coming. Don't know what it is, but it be big."

Detective Louis kept his head down the rest of the day. Didn't speak unless spoken to. He kept a mental head count of customers and the average sale and he knew somebody was getting rich. Multiplied by dozens of street corners, that figure was worth fighting for, worth killing for. He knew why the Zombies didn't want to give up any territory and why the Russians wanted to horn in.

Before leaving for the day, the dealer asked, "You got a cell phone?" He obviously didn't think everyone on the street would have one.

Louis said "Course," like it was the dumbest question ever. He'd have to control his reaction though, remember to not act like things that were normal in his world were normal to everyone. Everybody on the street didn't have a cellphone, or even shoes or didn't eat everyday.

"Gimme the digits."

Louis complied, thankful he'd memorized the number of the crappy, years-old, flip-phone, Detective Maloney'd given him. It wouldn't do for a Zombie to see him with his iPhone 6s Plus. That'd set off red flags everywhere. No way your typical street-dweller could afford one of those. The dealer's was probably a burner. Funny in a street way—his, from Maloney, was a piece of shit flip phone with a shattered screen that nobody would have in the twenty-first century and the dealer's was most likely a burner.

***

Louis was debriefing Musso and Maloney at the end of the shift.

"Talking to my 'supervisor' today. He says something big's getting ready to go down between the Zombies and the Russians."

"Yeah, that's what we hear," said Maloney.

"S' he have any idea what?"said Musso.

"No, man. He's a peon. Said so himself. What he said was "He just hears stuff.""

Maloney, always the optimist, said, "Well, keep your ears open and if you find out anything else, you know what to do."

"Call the cavalry."

"You got it."

Maloney said, "Wanna get a beer? The Pound?"

Louis said, "I wouldn't say 'no' to a beer."

"What about me?" Musso said, feigning hurt feelings.

"I didn't have to ask you. I knew you'd want one."

"True dat."

"Dude, I've told you," Maloney busted. "Don't use the ghetto talk. It doesn't fit you. You cannot pull it off."

"Yeah? Fuck you, then. How does that work for you?" But he said it with a huge smile.

"Now, now, boys," Louis said, "We don't want any hurt feelings."

"Aw, don't give Rocky a hard time," Maloney said. "He really isn't a bad guy. He just can't help himself.

"Yeah, but you guys are supposed to set a good example, show us the ropes. Y'all shouldn't be arguing," said Hernandez, his tongue firmly planted in cheek.

Maloney could tell the kids were going to be okay. Yeah, they could take care of themselves. Give as good as they got.

***

The Dog Pound was dead on this night.

"Rock, Johnny, how you doin?" Said Brendan, "Brought the new guys with you, I see.

"Got to break em in right," said Musso, "Lemme have a Gun Hill."

"You got it."

Although taking in the entire bar, as if noticing it for the first time, Johnny watched in happy anticipation as Brendan poured the beers.

Brendan returned with the Gun Hill and also a Guinness with the usual thick head for John, without him asking.

"What do the kids want?" he asked.

Hernandez, with some of the Filipino machismo the males were famous for, said, "Kids? I'll show you kids. I carry a .40 cal., you know."

Maloney said, "Come on, Hernandez. Don't take everything so personal."

Straightening his collar and then his hair, using a gesture that made him look like an Asian Nicholas Cage, he said, "I'm cool. I'm cool."

Maloney, trying to learn something about the new detectives—to bond with them a little, asked, "So, what kind of music you guys listen to?" Small talk to find out if he had anything in common with them."

Louis replied, " Well, Disturbed is one of my favorites and even if they have been around for awhile I still like Rage Against The Machine."

Hernandez said, "Even though I'm young I like classic rock and roll and old school pop. In the Philippines the most successful artists are cover bands for older American music. So we kind of grow up listening to those tunes. Oh, and most Filipinos like Journey ever since a Filipino took the place of Steve Perry as the lead singer."

Musso shook his head. "There hasn't been any real music made since Led Zeppelin."

"You're doing it again, Rock. I've told you about showing your age."

"Okay, Mr. Up-on-all-the-latest, what are you listening to?"

"I just downloaded the latest from Death Cab for Cutie. And I also like Disturbed."

"Death Cab For Cutie?...What the hell is that?...Did they get that from New York City taxi drivers?...Downloaded?...What the fuck does that mean?..And Disturbed—is that a band or your condition?" Maloney really didn't believe Musso was that obtuse. He knew his partner was just exaggerating for effect, to make them think he was older and more out of touch than he really was. It was just part of his carefully crafted image.

TransSiberian Orchestra, not the Pound's typical music, famous for their original rock and roll Christmas music and pyrotechnics, played on the sound system, and knowing talking current music was a dead end with his partner, Maloney changed the subject and asked, "So Hernandez, is Christmas popular in the Philippines?"

The young Filipino seemed genuinely surprised at the question. "Are you kidding? The Philippines is overwhelmingly Catholic. We truly celebrate the holiday. Christmas music starts playing on radio and in malls on September first and continues until January. Most people put up trees in September as well. What we like to say is we celebrate Christmas in all the BER months—Septem*ber*, Octo*ber*, Novem*ber*, Decem*ber*," as he ticked them off on his fingers. "I would say the Philippines is more pro-Christmas than almost all other countries." Hernandez, had been an altar boy when younger and had even considered the priesthood, until he discovered he liked girls too much. "And did you know that the Philippines even celebrates the US Thanksgiving?"

Maloney was truly amazed. "Really? I would never have guessed that."

"Yeah, because of all the US Military men stationed there who marry hot Filipinas and stay, the country recognizes it, complete with turkey and all the trimmings. You need to get out of New York occasionally, John. Expand your frame of reference."

Everyone kidded Maloney about his lack of knowledge about anything not New York City. A lifelong New Yorker, he admitted his knowledge of other cultures was lacking. And most New Yorkers were kind of arrogant like that. If you weren't from New York, you weren't shit. John said, "If I weren't married, I'd have to check out some of those hot Filipinas."

After three rounds they had run out of stories and tired of telling lies. Musso said, "Rosalie will have my Italian ass if I'm late again. She's sick of smelling beer on my breath when I get home."

Maloney said, "Better than garlic."

"That was borderline racist."

"Not racist if it's true."

"Now, that really was racist."

Maloney just waved him off, dismissing him.

Hernandez and Louis called for their bar tabs at the same time. Louis said, "I think it's time we take our leave."

***

Rev told Marquise, "I think Five-0 will be less focused on us for a while."

"What makes you think that?"

"Can't say. Just a feeling."

"That's cool. Hope you're right."

"Well, you know how my intuitions are. I think you can count on it."

"We all trust your gut, boss. And by the way, I brought a new guy on yesterday and I'm looking at a couple more."

"Good, cool. Remember, we're in the people business. We may provide a product, but with inferior people the product won't sell itself." In fact, finding dependable people was their biggest challenge since most of the kids that would be interested in being a corner dealer were a product of broken homes or had spent significant time with DFACS.

"I know, boss. It's your mantra and we've all bought in to it."

***

Detective Hernandez's plan worked out as he'd hoped when a

dealer asked him if he wanted to run his own business, which led to a meeting with Marquise. The light-skinned brother wore dreads woven with red-and-white plastic beads halfway down his back. A cigarillo decorated the corner of his narrow mouth. He pretended that it pissed him off when friends called him Captain due to his resemblance to Captain Jack Sparrow, the Johnny Depp character in*Pirates Of The Caribbean*, when in truth he thought it was cool, because he'd say he was just keeping it real. But everyone who knew him knew he was cooler than the other side of the pillow.

"Dude," the dealer mouthed around the cig, "Sup?"

"Sup."

"Some Chuck Norris?" The dealer used one of the slang terms teenagers used for cocaine.

"I'm aiight."

"Chu hangin' 'round fo?"

"Ain't hanging around. Lookin' for a business opp."

"Kind of opp?"

"You know—my own corner."

"Want me to set up a meetin'?"

Still playing it cool, Hernandez said, "IDK. Possibly."

He decided that was enough, fist-bumped the dealer, left him hanging, then went around the corner to get a cup of coffee.

A large cup later, he returned. Acted like the corner was just a place he had to pass on the way to where he was going. The cocky swagger of an urban street Asian came to him naturally.

"So, you wanna' meetin'?"

"I don't know. Kinda busy."

"What's your name anyway?"

"They call me Jun—short for junior. Never have liked junior. My ole man was an asshole." Poured on the machismo Filipino men were known for.

When he finally relented and agreed to return the next morning for an interview with Marquise, he acted like he was doing the dealer a favor. At the meeting however, he toned down the cockiness, showing Marquise the respect his position with the Zombies deserved. Marquise said, "Let's get a cup of coffee," and they went to the same shop Jun had visited the previous day.

"So, why you want to be in the Zombies?"

"Well sir, if I'd had good sense I would've stayed in school, then I'd have a good job at Home Depot, or Macy's, but I thought I knew it all and now I'm paying for it. I just need the money. But I'll work real hard."

"I believe you, Jun. I think you have the personality for it. I'll give you a chance, but you have to show up on time and do what you need to do."

"Thank you, sir. I will." They finished their coffee while breaking down the previous weekend's Knicks game, which Hernandez could talk about, because he now was a New Yorker, even if most Filipinos were fans of west coast teams only because California was closer to the Philippines and those teams were on Filipino television more often.

He would start the next day.

***

"I'm on board," a wide-smiling Hernandez told Musso. "Start tomorrow."

"Good job," said Musso. "John will be right back. You can tell us both about it."

Once Maloney returned from Lou's office, Musso said, "The other kid got in with the Zombies. He wants to tell us about it." Musso's obvious enthusiasm for their plan coming together belied his use of the derogatory term "kid". He really didn't mean anything by it. Just Musso being Musso. Maloney said, "Lou had to leave early. Let's use his office."

They were still being careful about revealing their plan. Upon entering the glass front office, Maloney sat in the lieutenant's chair while Musso studied a wall of books, mostly non-fiction—police manuals, law enforcement procedurals with a handful of crime novels mixed in. Hernandez sat in a stiff-backed chair in front of the desk. If the lieutenant called anyone on the carpet he didn't want them to be comfortable.

"So, tell us what happened," said Maloney.

"Well, I made contact with a corner dealer, played it cool, didn't want to appear over-eager, and he arranged an interview for me with a big shot, maybe the man himself. Name's Marquise."

"Cool, but he's not the main man," said Musso, trying to appear disinterested, not looking away from the shelf of books as he interjected, but feeling the need to contribute. "The main man goes by Rev. Nobody's ever seen him. He wouldn't interview a dealer. The man's a ghost."

Maloney said, "Detective Musso's right. We know that much about him. This Marquise is probably upper management, though—a pretty big fish. We'll need you to give the sketch artist a description of him."

"That's easy. As big as a house and a shiny shaved head the size of a medicine ball."

Maloney said, "So when do you start?"

"In the a.m."

"Good, between you and Louis maybe we can finally make some headway on this thing."

"Count on it."

***

Hernandez and Louis were on their respective corners at 8 o'clock the next morning. The early-morning drug business rush had ended and, after a few days on the job, and confident that Louis was coming along, his trainer told him he was going to get a soda at the bodega around the corner. He figured the newbie could handle it by himself for five minutes.

A young kid—midteens—approached. Dug into his pocket and, instead of pulling out money, withdrew a rusty old switchblade. The button used to flick the blade didn't work, so he opened it and fixed it by hand.

"Gimme yo' money and all the foo-foo," said the youngster.

"Kid, I used to be you and believe me you don't want to do this," Detective Louis said. "I don't want to hurt you and I sure as hell don't want you to hurt me."

"Don't tell me what I don't wanna do."

"Kid, please, drop the knife, walk away, and we'll forget this happened."

"Forget yo' momma. Gimme the seven-up and yo' money."

"Ain't happenin', bro. And you'll thank me for this later."

The kid lunged at Louis, targeting his stomach with the sorry excuse for a knife. And in way less time than it would take Louis to write up the incident report, he side-stepped to his left and deflected it with his left inner arm in a cross-body downward sloping arc, then grabbing the kid's knife-hand with his own right, doubled him over backwards and, deciding it would be an unserious but memorable lesson for a kid who made a bad decision, bent his index finger backward, until he felt and heard it break, fracturing it in two places.

The kid howled in pain. "What'd you do that for?"

"What for? Are you really as dumb as you sound? I did it to keep you from hurting me, and make you think twice before you try anything like that again. I used to be stupid, too. Believe me, it's for your own good."

"Yeah, well fuck you, man," he said as he backed away clutching his injured hand to his stomach, and even though it was painful to do so, broke into a run. Louis weighed not telling his trainer what had happened, but then he figured it couldn't hurt to let the Zombies know he'd saved their money *and* their product. Moments later the trainer returned. "Anything happen while I was gone?"

"Nothing 'cept some kid tried to rob me."

"Rob you!"

"Yeah. Wanted the money and the merch."

"What happened?"

"He pulled a knife on me and I broke his finger and sent his sorry black ass packing."

"Good work, then."

"Thanks," he said sheepishly, but thought to himself, a NYC detective should be able to handle a fifteen-year-old with a knife. If he couldn't, he shouldn't be on the job.

***

Arriving back at Fort Apache, Louis had to do paperwork on the incident, just in case there was any backlash. One never knew. Even when their plan was over, if the kid or the kid's mom found out he was a cop, there would probably be a lawsuit, so he had to try to cover the department's collective asses by doing the required paperwork.

He completed the official forms and instead of putting them in Lou's inbox handed them directly to him. Something about them caught the lieutenant's eye and he scanned them right then. He picked up a red marker and holding it in his left hand, highlighted something he wanted to remember. He rubbed his temples, obviously stressed.

"Interesting reading," he said, dropping the papers on his desk. "Sounds like you handled it pretty well, though."

"Thanks, Lou. I'm sorry I had to hurt the kid. I really didn't want to."

"I know, but I don't need one of my detectives getting hurt...or worse. That would be a shit-storm of biblical proportions." He made the sign of the cross, a funny gesture since he was Jewish.

"I hear you, and my moms wouldn't be real happy about it, either."

***

Louis and Hernandez decided to have a quick one at the Pound.

Maloney and Musso heard the bell over the door jingle and saw the rooks enter. They called them over to join them at their usual spot at the bar.

Musso said to Louis, "I think we should call *you* Rocky from now on."

"Oh, mother...I didn't think the lieutenant would say anything."

"Yeah, right, Lou can't hold his water, besides," Maloney said, "this is big news. Everybody needs to know when one of New York's finest defends his honor. You defended all of us. What you did will prevent future attacks on citizens and cops."

"He was just a kid. I didn't even break a sweat, and I regret breaking his finger."

Musso said, "We heard it was his arm."

"And a leg," said Maloney.

"Man, you two need to give a brother a break."

"Like you did the kid? We'll give you a break when you have a few years under your belt." Musso was enjoying it a little too much.

Hernandez shook his head, but being Louis' partner and best friend he was enjoying it too. Musso made up with Louis by buying them all a cold mug and offering a respectful toast. "To our newest badass and a young man who is going to be a damn fine detective. To Mo..." And he raised his mug. Maloney and Hernandez joined in. "To Mo."

It was a precinct tradition to honor them when anyone did something above and beyond the call of duty. And what Detective Louis did definitely called for it. He was truly humbled, and embarrassed. And if he were honest his eyes got a little moist. He knew his father, just retired from walking a beat, when he told him, would be bursting with pride for him.

They finished the first round and Louis said, "That's it for me. Got to be on the street early."

Hernandez agreed. "Yeah, we're working stiffs now. Let's do it." Musso and Maloney decided they'd have one more.

After the new guys left Maloney said, "That was a real nice gesture, Rock."

"What? The toast? It was nothing. He deserved it."

"Anyways, it was a nice gesture coming from a crusty old curmudgeon like you."

"Watch it. You're skating on thin ice."

Chapter Eleven
Prelude to War

"Something's up," said Marquise to Tommy. Tommy could tell by his tone that it was serious and he cut off the song he was singing in the middle of the word, *mine*. It was a Lou Rawls standard. The quizzical look Tommy shot Marquise begged the question, "what" without saying a word.

"We don't know. Just keep your eyes and ears open. But, I have a feeling—just a feeling, mind you—that the goddamn Russians are planning to hit us." Marquise wouldn't deliver a personal message to each of his dealers, but truth was, Tommy was his favorite and he was worried something might happen to him if anything big went down. He'd hate it for Tommy's mom and his younger brother and sister.

Detective Hernandez had overheard the brief but ominous conversation. But, hearing police sirens a couple of blocks away, he couldn't worry about that right now. He hoped that his brothers-in-blue didn't need him. Unable to wear a radio while undercover, he could only wonder what could be happening.

Hernandez clenched his fists and gritted his teeth against the mental pain caused by his lack of knowledge, and quickly decided that this was the worst part of undercover work—being unable to join in when he might be needed.

***

Saturday arrived and MC and Johnny, dressed-to-the-nines because that's what New Yorkers did at Christmas time, took a taxi to the midtown location of Radio City Music Hall. MC borrowed her mother's car-length mink coat for the early December frosty weather and Johnny wore a Ralph Lauren black worsted wool single-breasted overcoat over a dark gray suit and a fedora for protection against the chill night air. He'd bought the overcoat at an outlet store in New Jersey at a huge discount.

By 5:30 in December New York would be full dark and the temperature steadily dropping. A diamond ring Johnny wore belonged to his father but he'd asked him if he could have it before the ravages of Alzheimer's caused him to forget that junior wanted it, or even remember who junior was.

The couple exited the cab at the Avenue of the Americas—the official name of what New Yorkers call 6th Avenue—main entrance. A line of people four abreast was queued up on three sides of the block waiting to enter. The doors would open an hour before curtain but if one didn't arrive early you risked missing the opening scene due to the throng. Everyone's, natives and tourists alike, favorite song in the show was *A New York Christmas* and no one wanted to risk missing it.

Johnny, unable to leave the job at the office, thought about how this would be a horrific location for terrorists to strike at Christmastime in America's greatest city. A family, with two small daughters, a pair about ages two and four, in matching outfits of red velvet, had eyes shining with excitement knowing that the favorite holiday of all children was a mere three weeks away. The younger of the two looked at Johnny and said, "Hey man."

Johnny squatted down and said, "Hello, darling.

MC looked at them, wistfully. "Aren't they the most precious things you've ever seen?"

Distracted as he was by all the activity on the sidewalk—the policeman in his soul—he found it hard to focus on the children, but had to admit, "Definitely. And did you hear how articulate she was? Hey, man?" Johnny thought they were very precious, indeed. He knew MC wanted children, and soon. And he wanted what she wanted.

"As soon as I graduate and get a job as an attorney we can start trying," he said. He would enjoy the trying.

But first he wanted to be off the job so MC wouldn't have anything else to worry about. She rose up on tiptoes and gave him a kiss. Her head inclined, the lights reflecting from above the grand old theatre sparkled in her eyes. Johnny smelled his favorite perfume, Viktor & Rolf "Flowerbomb," the one that always made his pulse quicken.

Part Two
War

Chapter Twelve
Buildup

Early December and Arkady was anxious to exact revenge. The Christmas season, the season of peace and love in this country, would be the perfect time to strike. He thought it would be ironic because peace and love were not emotions he often pondered. His anxiety manifested itself by chain-smoking two packs of unfiltered cigarettes and drinking almost a fifth of Russian vodka a day.

Unfiltered cigarettes had killed his father. Lung cancer caused him to drop from a solid two-hundred, twenty-five pounds to a deathly–looking ninety before he finally succumbed.

Arkady had never smoked until now. He'd always said he'd never take up the habit that killed his revered father. But when conflict with the Zombies erupted, nurture and his genetics won the battle with his typical good sense.

His thoughts were on a subset of firearms called assault weapons by American politicians but were rifles, semi automatic rifles—America's political correctness would eventually be its downfall; it used to be tough, like Russia, but not anymore. Some could be converted to automatic, and it was surprisingly easy for a mechanic, a hobbyist, or a handyman, anyone experienced with tools and a basic knowledge of mechanics.

The Russian's storehouse currently held fifty such weapons—one for each man—now in his gang—but he hoped for more to arrive with the men expected from the motherland.

***

DeAngelo keyed in the number he'd been given for Detective Maloney.

"The Zombies be opening up a new corner."

"Talk to me," Maloney said. DeAngelo gave him the location of the new corner and told him as soon as possible would be a good time to strike.

***

Maloney changed into the businessman's costume he kept stashed in his locker: Gray pin-stripe suit, not too expensive, white starched cotton dress shirt from Lands End, red power tie with dove gray dolphins in a diagonal rep pattern. A pocket square matching the tie, insouciantly placed into the jacket breast pocket provided the finished look of a young urban professional. To complete the ensemble he slipped into black leather Ecco dress shoes with a soft sole he could run in if needed. After tucking the shirt and knotting the necktie into a half-Windsor he slipped his Glock Model 19 into a Bianchi leather holster onto his belt on the right hip. The black leather holster matched his Eccos but didn't cost nearly as much even though the leather was glove soft and far more comfortable than the typical concealed carry rig. Unseen and undetectable under his clothing was a small but powerful microphone that would transmit everything said by Maloney and the dealer directly into the Bluetooth earbuds worn by Musso and the others. They would know precisely when to leap into action.

Musso, said, "You know, you look like a user. You ready?"

"Yeah. Shoot me up. Since I'm depending on you to cover my ass, the most important question is, are *you* ready."

"Always. You know I don't want to have to tell MC if anything were to happen to her baby. And the other guys are ready, too."

"You're damn right. The last thing you want to do is to have to explain to her how you let me get killed."

It's well documented that Irishmen are known for their tempers, but what isn't as well known is one wouldn't want to get on the bad side of an Irish woman either.

Two other teams were set to help Musso with protection if needed. They weren't concerned, though. Taking down one young drug dealer should be easy enough.

To be less conspicuous Musso and Maloney drove in Musso's personal vehicle, a several year old beige Chevy pickup, he sometimes used in undercover situations because it was almost invisible. The other detectives followed well behind in unmarked cruisers. Musso would let Maloney out on a side street and give him time to get to the corner on foot, timing his arrival seconds after the takedown. The backups' arrival would be seconds after his. They'd practiced this play many times.

Musso pulled to the curb to let Maloney out. "Okay, partner, good luck."

"Thanks, just don't leave me hanging."

"Wouldn't dare, and just for a final mic check say something as soon as you get out."

Maloney exited the car, took a few steps and spoke, "One small step for man..." and glanced over his shoulder to see if his best friend heard him.

Musso, grinning through the windshield, gave him a thumbs up. Maloney acknowledged it with a grin and a two-finger salute. He headed off down the sidewalk, not strolling, but not on a mission either. Kind of an easy businessman's stride. With a purpose.

***

Detective Louis, now known as Mo on the corner, was bored. Apparently, dealing drugs was a routine job, at least most of the time. Nothing remotely adrenaline raising had happened since he encountered the punk with the knife. He had to admit, he'd had a momentary rush when he realized what was happening, but then his training took over and he controlled the spike and what could have become ugly.

His dealer-supervisor had indicated that in a couple more days he'd probably get his own corner.

***

Maloney approached the corner that deAngelo had indicated was the Zombies' newest. Spotted the dealer. Dude didn't even attempt to hide what he was doing.

As he neared, the dealer caught his eye. "Hey, boss man, looks like you could use a little pick me up."

"Good eye," said Maloney. "Rough morning at the office."

"You ain't no cop, is you?"

"Wearing a a suit that sells for a thousand bills? Yeah right." He'd picked it up on sale at Lands End for less than a buck and a quarter. And, the department had reimbursed him. He was counting on the ignorance of the young sidewalk dealer to be unable to tell the difference.

"Okay, cool. I had to ask."

Maloney knew most dealers believed if they asked if you were a cop you had to tell the truth or the arrest wouldn't stand up. What most were too stupid to know was that if they had drugs on them nothing else mattered. The dealer pulled out the merch and said, "Five bills."

Maloney appeared to reach for a billfold but his hand wrapped around the stock of his weapon while the other withdrew his gold shield from the inside breast pocket of the cheap suit jacket.

"Freeze," he shouted as Musso screeched to a stop, his truck door flying open wide to provide generous cover. Musso dropped behind it while withdrawing his weapon and landing in an aggressive firing position using the vee between the door window and the car frame to support his gun hand. Scared shitless, the dealer dropped the product to the cracked sidewalk before freezing, but freeze he did, eyes agape like open camera lenses absorbing light. Backup arrived less than five seconds later for a total of six detectives for the arrest of one kid.

Noticing a wet spot spreading across the front of the dealer's pants, Maloney felt sorry for the young man, who couldn't have been long out of high school, if he'd finished at all.

***

In an interview cell at Fort Apache, Maloney said, "Gerald, As we like to say in the country, you're up shit creek." Funny because Maloney was New York City born-and-bred, and had never even ventured into the country, and the only wild animals he'd ever seen were in cages at the Bronx Zoo.

Maloney counted off the man's problems."One, intent to sell; two, more than three grams; three, within one thousand feet of a school or family housing complex. You hit the trifecta, my man." Adding in his best imitation gameshow host voice: "What does he win, Detective Musso? Class A felony…minimum twenty years!" Then, pointing a thumb in his partner's direction, adding in his normal voice: "You'll be almost as old as him when you get out,"

"Oh, and a ten-thousand-dollar fine," Maloney finished. "Only way you can help yourself is to talk your ass off. Who's the boss? The head man? Where do we find him? Give us everything you got. Now!"

Small-time drug dealer Gerald Whitman was sacred to death, on the verge of tears, pleading. "Sir, I don't know who he is. Nobody know the man. Don't even know what he look like. Don't know anybody who know what he look like."

"Well, you better find somebody who knows what he looks like," Maloney said, " because you need help."

Musso grunted, his patience wearing thin. "This is getting us nowhere."

Maloney expelled a big breath, and, with an effort that made it appear it weighed a hundred pounds, picked up his iPad.

"I guess you're right, partner. But I'd hoped that Gerald could help himself."

***

The Rev's cell rang. MC Hammer's "U Can't Touch This"

"Marquise," Rev said, " Talk to me."

"We lost Gerald, Gerald Whitman."

"What?" Rev didn't sound surprised, just curious.

"Yeah, the pigs busted him an hour and a half ago."

"Damn. What else?"

"Early morning, so they probably got six grams."

"Damn." Wasn't much but he still wasn't happy about it. It was just a cost of running a business. He didn't like it for Gerald or his family, but in the long run it might be beneficial to the Zombies.

"You know what to do now, right?" Rev asked Marquise.

"The usual, for moms—five hundred dollars tucked in a gift basket of food?"

"Make it a thousand, this time."

"Whatever you say, Rev."

Marquise thought, *man this one must really bother the boss.* He was glad to see that. He'd have to let the other salesmen know. It'd build loyalty, knowing their families aren't forgotten. Most gang leaders don't care about their people like Rev does. Unable to offer perks like insurance, doing something like this was big. He just didn't know the reason it bothered Rev so much. Marquise arrived at the corner where Detective Louis apprenticed.

"The cops took down our new corner on 222nd St.", he said to the trainer. "So keep your eyes open. If you notice anyone, if you get a whiff of anyone who even hints at the smell of bacon, get the hell outta here double time."

"Will do, Marquise. How'd it happen?"

"Don't have the details yet. Have to wait til our attorneys talk to him. Until then, stay on your toes. We can't afford to lose any more men or product."

Hearing the exchange, Louis wondered was why the detectives didn't tip him the bust was going down. He decided it must have been a spur-of-the-moment takedown.

***

Arkady's top lieutenants had their marching orders. Find more automatic weapons locally, even though their preferred Russian-made tools were impossible to acquire through the usual channels.

Boris and Vladimir knew they were screwed if they didn't acquire fifty additional assault weapons. Arkady had given them a literal blank check. Failure would be unforgivable. The Romanians operated out of Queens, and Boris and Vladimir heard through the thug grapevine that they had a weapons cache much the size of their own so, remembering the ancient proverb—the enemy of my enemy is my friend—they turned to their longtime enemies and asshole buddies and secured a meeting with a pair of Romanian lieutenants.

To get to Queens from the Bronx they had to take two different buses, The 6 and the E. Depending on the time of day, and assuming they didn't stop at a bar for a couple of vodkas, the trip could take anywhere from forty-five minutes to an hour and a quarter . If they negotiated a buy they would return in a panel truck to pick up the weapons.

They arrived at a nondescript warehouse much like their own that served as the Romanians' headquarters. Neither the Russians or the Romanians had the good sense of la Cosa Nostra to meet in the private dining rooms of Italian restaurants where at least they could dine on copious amounts of pasta and drink good Italian Chianti while they met.

Looking at Constantin and Nicolae was like looking into a mirror for Boris and Vladimir. Hard men, used up, nothing left for anything but killing. In a thick, Eastern European accent, Nicolae said, "So, you need weapons."

It wasn't a question.

"Yes, and we have—how do you say—funds."

"Good. You will need them," Constantin grinned. "But first, what for do you need these fine weapons of ours?"

Boris and Vladimir had anticipated this question:"Spare parts."

They couldn't have word reach the streets that they were planning an assault on the Zombies. That could make all comers think the time ripe for a takeover of their own.

Nicolae: "Parts?" He gazed toward the paint-flaked ceiling as he pondered. He wasn't buying it.

The Romanians weren't stupid, but as long as the Russians stuck to their story it didn't matter what the Romanians thought. Even though anyone with common sense—and the Romanians had common sense—could figure out what they needed them for even if they didn't know against whom—they wouldn't *know*.

Nicolae nodded at Constantin and the younger man spoke. "Okay—fifty weapons—one hundred thousand US dollars. No check. No direct deposit. How you say? Cash on the barrel-head."

That was grand larceny. But everyone in the room was a crook, so they hadn't expected anything less. They'd figured street value at a thousand bucks per weapon, so they expected to pay a fifty percent premium, but a hundred percent was highway robbery. Vladimir responded. "We'll have to run it by the boss. Give us your phone numbers." And like legitimate businessmen sitting around conference tables in meetings all over the city, they exchanged cell numbers, but these phones were burners, prepaid phones that all would ditch in a few days, for security's sake.

Nicolae said, "Okay, but don't—how do the Americans say—drag your feet, or this number won't work in a few days."

Boris said, "And you think ours will?" And they all laughed at themselves.

"Very good" Constantin said. "Then we understand each other."

Nods all around and Boris and Vladimir took their leave. They reversed their route on the bus line to the Bronx. This time they got off at the first shitty bar they found. Sauntered in and being Russian, ordered vodka. Didn't like being stereotyped but they couldn't help themselves. When you're from Russia you drink vodka. Or as the old saying goes, *When in Rome…*

***

Back at headquarters Arkady said, "Don't you dumb fucks pay attention? Like I told you. I don't give a shit what it costs. Get the goddamn guns."

He knew that whatever the cost, he'd make up the expense by using them to take the Zombies territory, so it made financial sense to him. In the legit world it would be considered a tax write-off for business.

Boris dialed the number Nicolae had given him.

"We got the okay." And after agreeing on a meeting time and fair play parameters, they were set to deliver the cash and pick up the weapons mid-morning the following day.

Next on the agenda for that night: Acquiring a panel truck in which to transport the weapons and a half dozen gunmen with high-powered firearms just to keep the Romanian assholes borderline honest. Carrying a hundred large around the Bronx and Queens was not something one did without serious firepower.

They decided to "borrow" a truck from a north Bronx lot where booted-and-towed vehicles were stored, usually for just a few days before their owners claimed them. This particular lot was rented by the city to hold vehicles impounded from an area of Manhattan north of Central Park and the Bronx. The tire repair shop next door had closed around dark. Not much activity in this industrial area in the Bronx at this time of night to concern them. There were several of the lots serving the five boroughs—one was even shared with part of New Jersey. The NYPD impounded thousands of cars a year. No one would notice if a crappy truck were missing for a day, or if they did, no one would give a shit—not even the vehicle's owner.

They'd scouted the lot in the daytime and decided on a target: A non-descript white panel truck that had a faded ABA Supplies logo on both sides. That business probably didn't exist anymore and whoever owned the truck now probably didn't care he was providing the defunct company with free advertising.

During the night, Boris, Vladimir and two of their comrades-in-arms visited the lot which wore none of the festive yuletide decorations beginning to dress the rest of the city. The men wore all black. Black shoe polish hid their faces. On a mission requiring stealth, they waited until after midnight. They didn't carry guns because, if they were caught, they didn't want weapons charges on top of the relatively minor offense of breaking and entering.

The common term "junkyard dog" was used because it's real. And on this night they encountered not one, but two. Sharp-toothed Doberman pincers. They came prepared with large-boned raw steak to keep any canines busy. They threw the meat over the fence on the other side of the lot from the gate where they worked on the lock and chain with bolt cutters. The lock was snapped in seconds by the strongest henchman.The lot was not well-lighted. Barring any hiccups they'd be able to snatch the truck in less than an hour.

The hiccup occurred when the dobies, tiring of the bones, raced around the corner of the building growling, white fangs flashing in the moonlight. If one's imagination ran toward fiction, they would be rabid. Boris and Vladimir made it into the cab of the truck and the two henchmen scrambled into the rear and slammed the door. As it crashed to the truck floor it landed mid-body on one of the vicious animals. He was silenced after a pitiful yelp, front-half in and rear-half out of the truck. They lifted the door mere inches and with a boot-covered foot shoved the lifeless animal into the dust of the darkened lot.

Fortunately the ancient truck's engine started right up even thought the oil light never went off. The tired vehicle's heater didn't work and in the early hours of morning they could see their breath in the cab. Driving slowly so as not to attract attention they got back to their warehouse headquarters at three a.m. And after naps on army-style cots in a backroom they arose in time to make it to Queens for their ten-o'clock meeting with the Romanians.

Seven o'clock show time and Boris and Vladimir jumped into the cab of the shitty truck while six of their lackeys, armed to the teeth, piled into the rear. The weapons of choice: various flavors of AR-15s— American Tactical Imports, Armalite, and Bushmaster were the best— but they'd make do with anything they could get their hands on in the secondary market. In addition to Vladimir's shotgun, both he and Boris wore holstered Makarov semi-auto pistols chambered for .380 ACP.

Driving from the Bronx to the Romanians' warehouse near LaGuardia, wasn't that far in miles, probably less than ten, but during the New York City morning rush hour it could take every bit of the three hours they'd allotted. Both the cab and cargo areas smelled of diesel fuel.

Their destination, a nondescript warehouse-industrial complex like the sort in every large city in the country, popular because of airport proximity, chosen by the Romanians for its remoteness from anyone who would care about what went on behind the warehouse doors. When they neared the complex Boris punched in the number of one of the Romanians' throwaway phones they had called before. "Yeah—one minute," he said, curtly.

"We're here," was the taut response from one of their comradely enemies. Nicolae turned to Constantin and even though the Russians were early—it wasn't yet ten o'clock—said, "It's about goddamn time." Due to frayed nerves.

As they approached 719, the metal door rolled up. As the worn out panel truck pulled in, Vladimir, riding shotgun, leaped down from the cab, arcing the business end of a twelve-gauge in a semi-circle around his body; the truck's rear door rose and the six lackeys emerged, their weapons at the ready. Their clothes held the stench of diesel fuel from the long drive enclosed in the truck. The first one breathed in the stale air of the warehouse to try and clear the diesel fuel from his head, and coughed deeply.

"Damn. It's good to get out of there," he said to no one. "I need some goddamn air."

The Romanians had their own twelve gunmen and although they greatly outnumbered the Russians, no one wanted to start something that wouldn't end well for anyone.

Constantin emerged from an old office door holding a frosted pane of glass that rattled when it shut.

"Hello, my friends," he said in a thick Eastern European accent. "It seems we have the same healthy distrust of each other. It will—how you say—keep us honest. And what's the other saying? Honor among thieves? These Goddamn Americans—they have a way with the words, yes? How else could they give the world Edgar Allen Poe?"

His jovial manner belied the seriousness of the next few minutes. They would all be happy if the deal could be consummated with everyone going home alive.

"You have the money?"

"Ya, you have the weapons?"

"Of course. They're always here, but you had to arrive with the money. It appears there has to be some trust."

Constantin signaled one of his men. Another aluminum garage door rolled up and a golf cart belching smoke, pulling a trailer, emerged. The driver pulled up next to Constantin so closely that he could reach in without moving his feet. Without even looking in, the first weapon he touched and withdrew was a no-name AR-15. Vlad hoped the rest were of better quality.

He motioned for Vladimir and Boris to come over. As they neared he withdrew a second weapon and tossed one to each of them. They examined each weapon—dry firing, testing the action and sighting down the fixed sights. Each of them leveled the weapon, in the direction of the Romanian leader, who didn't react other than to say, "So, what do you think, my friends?" with his arms lowered forty-five degrees from his body and his palms turned out and extended in peaceful supplication.

Boris gave a short, terse nod, Vladimir gestured for their henchmen to form a semicircle with their backs to the passenger door, weapons at the ready, as the pair returned to the cab. They retrieved a small black nylon backpack and in what was obviously a well-thought out plan, tossed it over the heads of their gunmen to the concrete floor.

Their armed guard was prepared for this, and didn't react to the bag flying over their heads and landing heavily in front of them. Except for their less-than-military-like physical condition, one might have thought them a well-disciplined fighting unit.

Constantin picked up the backpack containing a couple bricks of Ben Franklins. Took it to the glass-doored office from which he'd emerged and motioned for the Russians to join him. It wouldn't take three of his moneymen long to count a thousand one-hundred-dollar bills. Dividing the money into three roughly equal stacks, they looked like cashiers at a horse track or a Vegas casino with the speed at which they thumbed the dead founding fathers.

Constantin offered Vladimir and Boris tea while they waited for the men to finish their count. V and B declined but were impressed by that small gesture. Russians had always thought Romanians uncivilized at best and untamed animals at worst, and that little offering served to change their opinion—of these Romanians, at least, if not all.

Constantin poured himself a cup: a formal China vessel with pale-green flowers edging the stark white cup and saucer. By the time he'd finished his second, the two Russians ever vigilant, his moneymen had finished counting and proclaimed the amount accurate. One hundred thousand US dollars.

He rose and said, "It's a pleasure doing business with you."

Unsmiling, Vladimir and Boris nodded. Their stoicism belied the fact that their opinion of their asshole buddies had changed. They exited the small office covered by their six gunmen as they immediately returned to the cab of the truck. The six loaded their haul.

The return drive to the Bronx was not nearly as tension-filled as that to Flushing, Queens. Accomplishing their goal of acquiring the needed weapons and not having the 100K ripped off, or losing any men, would make Arkady happy, even if he wouldn't show it. Vladimir and Boris had been with him a long time and had known him for even longer, so they knew what to expect, and most of the time that was nothing. And if one expected nothing, it was hard to be disappointed.

***

Small-time drug dealer, Gerald Whitman was safely in jail. Musso and Maloney wouldn't have anything more to do with him until he went before the judge to be indicted. The fallout from the bust of a Zombie intensified the buzz on the street. No one knew if there was a connection, but it was like waiting for a terrorist to set off another bomb in Manhattan. Everyone was expecting something to happen between the Zombies and the Russians. But nobody knew what or when.

Musso and Maloney told Louis and Hernandez to meet them at the Pound that night. They hadn't talked in a few days—it had only been three but it felt like more—and Musso was getting nervous. He needed to know that they were on the same page and he wanted a debrief.

Musso and Maloney were standing at the bar. They watched as Hernandez and Louis entered, sidestepped a Christmas tree and made their way over. Louis tried to fist-bump Musso, but he wouldn't raise his fist, and left the kid hanging. Offended, Louis said, "Come on, man. I tried to pound you at the pound. Now, that's funny, Dude. What's the problem?"

"I've said it before. I'm a fifty-six-year-old white guy," Musso said. "I'm too old to do that street shit, and too tired."

Maloney said, "Come on, dude, give the kid a break."

Musso said, "Now, don't you start with me. I've told you about calling me "dude"."

Maloney put his hand on Louis' shoulder. "I'm sorry, my man, but don't try that with him. He really is too old, and too uncool. But don't hold it against him. He's never been cool. He just can't help it."

"What do you mean-never been cool?" Musso said, "I'm cool."

"Sure you are, partner."

It sounded condescending because it was.

Hernandez didn't wait for the senior detectives to question him. "Don't know what, but something big is going down," he said.

Louis agreed.

Hernandez sounded a little pissed, "Wait. Before we discuss that, how about you guys tell us why you didn't let us know about the bust. It would've been nice to know it was going down."

Louis was even more pissed off. "Yeah, that would have been helpful. I thought we worked together, even if we aren't partners."

Maloney, on the defensive, held up his hands palm out. "I can understand why you guys are upset, but we had to move fast and we actually thought we were protecting you. It was for your own good, we thought it would be better for you if you didn't know. We just didn't want you to be compromised."

"For our own good?" Hernandez asked. "What do you think we are, children? I thought we were NYPD detectives trained by the finest to *be* the finest."

Louis stood up and made his way toward the Pound's door. "This is bullshit." He put his hand on the knob and began to turn it. The reflection of Detective Musso rising behind him in the glass window of the wood door made him hesitate.

 "Detective Louis—Mo. You have a right to be pissed. It won't happen again and no more kid jokes, either. We're sorry. We made a bad decision."

"You're damn right you made a bad decision, *Detective*."

"Detective Musso's right," Maloney said. "We were wrong and it will not happen again."

Louis removed his hand from the door and mollified at least for the moment, turned back towards the bar. "Okay."

Maloney said, "All right, let's talk about what's happening with the Zombies."

Each of them momentarily nursed bruised egos, so getting started would go a little slower than they'd have liked. But Hernandez jumped in. "Well, like we said, I don't really know what it is but I can tell it's big because I see the the boss of the dealers nearly every day now. And he's warning us to be cautious. And if I can read an imprint or the pull on a jacket—and I can— he's carrying and he wasn't a few days ago."

Louis added. "Yeah, my trainer is about to piss his pants every time a customer approaches him. He's not usually that jumpy."

A little more talk was getting them nowhere. Maloney said, "I'm going to call DeAngelo. Maybe he knows something or can find out something."

"That's great," Musso said sarcastically,

"I get it. You don't like him, but we need to get on top of this. Something is going to happen and we need to find out what it is. He's our best bet."

"That's sad. That guy is our best bet."

Agreeing that Hernandez and Louis should go back to their corners and keep their eyes and ears open, Maloney moved to the other end of the bar for a little privacy to call DeAngelo's cell phone.

"Okay, we'll see you at nine in the a.m., then," he said.

Maloney returned to where the other detectives stood.

To Musso, he said, "We're meeting DeAngelo at The Hall of Fame at nine o'clock in the morning."

"The Hall of Fame?"

Maloney shrugged. "Yeah. He says he sleeps under a bridge near there sometime."

"Okay..."

"Meet me at the office at eight," Maloney said. "I want to make a stop on the way."

"No problem."

Good nights were exchanged and they stepped outside into the darkness.

***

They got in their cruiser Musso driving. Maloney said, "Pull through the Burger King on the south end of the Concourse." Musso turned left to go south on the wide boulevard. The traffic on the Grand Concourse on a Saturday morning was nothing short of insanity.

"What, MC didn't cook you breakfast this morning?"

"It's not for me."

"Oh," said Musso. He could guess what his partner was up to.

Maloney leaned across Musso to order two sausage burritos, hash browns and a large coffee.

Musso stared at him.

"What? I feel sorry for the guy."

"Great—my partner's becoming buddies with an asshole."

"We're not buddies, but I still think he can help us, so I don't think there's anything wrong with me helping him out a little."

Officer Maloney was also a fan of the Hall. Founded in 1900, the Hall of Fame sat on the campus of Bronx Community College, formerly the Bronx campus of New York University, high above most of the city. An outdoor hall, a colonnade with ninety-eight busts of celebrated Americans. Inventors, musicians, actors, generals, politicians, and the like. No one new had been elected to the Hall since 1976, so it was severely lacking in women, Hispanics and African-Americans. For most people it was now a forgotten piece of history. For most young people a completely unknown piece of history.

Musso parked the cruiser and after Maloney collected the bag of fast food and coffee from the back seat they strode toward the colonnade where they'd already spotted DeAngelo.

As they got closer, De gave them his trademark, *sup.*

Musso ignored him and looked away.

Maloney gave him the sack of food and De sheepishly dug through it and mumbled *thanks.*

In an attempt to make him feel less self conscious, Maloney said, "We already ate ours."

"Let's walk around," De said. "I'll eat as we look."

Then he added, "You know this place ain't very popular with the brothers because it ain't diverse." He took the lid off of the coffee and tossed it into a trash bin. He took a sip and steam rose from the cup, and mixing with his warm breath, rose into the cold wind coming off the Hudson River. "You know, it's mostly old dead white dudes. But I like it. These people are the ones who made this country great."

Musso, surprised, arched his eyebrows and said, "Hmmph, there's something we can agree on."

Maloney was just surprised that this young street black man, who in all likelihood probably wasn't well educated, would like a place like this, with the busts of, as he put it, all these old dead white guys. And appreciate the history of it. Maloney liked bringing out-of-town visitors here more than the more traditional sites New York was known for.

De, trying to take control, said, "So, you have some questions about the street."

Musso said, "We think something big is getting ready to happen."

"I do, too," said DeAngelo.

Musso got anxious, lost his cool. "So spill it. Goddamnit." Then, turning to his partner, said, "Getting anything from this guy is like pulling my goddamn molars."

Maloney, getting use to his role as mediator between Musso and De Angelo, said, "What do you think's happening, De?"

"I think," he said, pausing, either to piss off Musso or searching for words, "I think the goddamn Russians are getting ready to declare war on the Zombies."

Maloney, always the master of the understatement, said, "That's pretty big."

Musso whistled a two-beat note.

"Any idea when or where this could happen?" said Musso.

"None. You guys are the detectives. Detect."

Maloney said, "Touché." DeAngelo and his intelligent, dry wit were beginning to grow on him.

They wandered the Hall and talked an hour longer, not discovering anything else that seemed relevant, so they thanked DeAngelo, and said, "Can we give you a ride somewhere?"

"No thanks. No offense, but I can't see be seen with you guys. It could damage my reputation, you know, being seen with a couple of New York's more disreputable citizens."

Even Musso had to admit that was a funny line.

Getting back in the cruiser, Maloney said, "How about some lunch? Hard Rock Café at Yankee Stadium? I'm buying."

"No, thanks. I'd like to, but I've gotta take care of something."

"You're passing up a free lunch, with beer, at the Hard Rock?"

"Sorry, partner; this is important."

***

Monday morning and Maloney entered the double doors of Fort Apache. Greeted Sergeant Cabrera. As usual, Musso was already at his desk.

Maloney said, "What—in the hell— is that?"

"What," Musso said.

"What is that, in your ear?" He saw a small silver star.

"What? This? I had a pierced ear when I was young. Decided to try it again."

"So that's what you had to take care of Saturday, instead of lunch with me? And I'm to blame for it? I apologize. Totally. Completely. But bottom line is you got your feelings hurt when I said you were uncool and you acted out."

"What an ego. This isn't about you."

"That will be a permanent reminder to me that I should be careful about what I say. I take it back. I was wrong. You're cool. Now, get rid of that thing. If you take it out now the hole will grow back together

"No, I like it. I should have done this a long time ago."

"No, you shouldn't have."

***

The Rev had a runner go to Starbucks for carry-out and over venti lattes he and his inner circle sat down to discuss the tension they were all feeling.

Rev spread his arms wide and asked his inner circle, "What do you hear, my brothers?"

Darelle said, "Same thing you do, Rev. Something big's coming."

Harry said, "Yeah, and we better be ready."

"Amen," said Rev. Adding, "Darelle, do *you* think the Russians are getting ready to retaliate?"

"Yes, I do, boss."

"Does anybody have a guess as to when we should look for it?"

They all agreed that the closer it got to Christmas, about three weeks away, that they should be in condition red, on full alert.

Carmelito said, "Fuck. If those sons of bitches do something during Christ's birthday, I'll kick their asses myself. Those goddamn Russians don't have any faith. They don't believe in anything." Rev noticed that when each one of them spoke they gestured, in emphasis. He liked that. He took it as a sign of intellect.

"So we're in agreement," Rev said. "It's coming. Reach out to people you know. Ask for any help from your contacts. Knowledge is power. We have to be prepared. Like the Boy Scouts."

"Yeah," Harry said. "But fight like the fucking US Marines."

The others liked that and showed their agreement with a chorus of *oorahs* filling the dining room.

***

Arkady spoke to his lieutenants. Eight hard men. Men who had long ago given up the dreams of younger men. Career criminals. Men who were content to live out their years being what they were— soldiers—soldiers with no ideals, no moral code, no sense of honor. Their only loyalty to themselves, money their guiding light, the focal point that brought them together and, as long as they kept their eye on the prize, the only thing that would keep them together. The only thing that could keep them from turning on each other.

"Comrades, our time nears. The holiday, the birth of their king, approaches. The Silent Night, the night of Joy To The World, is when we strike. A fitting time for us to take our rightful place here in the Bronx. Thanks to Vladimir and Boris we have fifty new rifles and I am expecting fifty new men to arrive from our glorious motherland over the next ten days and we will be ready for our mission."

***

Monday morning and Marquise showed up to tell Mo he was getting his own corner. It seemed that when he saved the Zombies' merch and cash with the way he handled the young punk who'd tried to jack him up it had put him on a fast-track. He was getting his reward. Moving a couple of blocks west and about a half-mile north. It would be a good corner.

"Thanks, Marquise. I'll do a good job."

"You better," was the terse reply from Marquis, who added, "We don't hire losers in the Zombies, and I vouched for you. So you mess up and you've got to answer to me."

"I hear you," said Mo. Even though he was a well-trained NYPD detective skilled in self-defense and pugilism, he didn't think he'd want to take on Marquise *mano-a-mano*. The big man was close to a foot taller and probably outweighed him by a hundred, a hundred twenty-five pounds.

Marquis and Mo got in the big man's large Cadillac SUV for the ten-minute ride in Bronx traffic. The big vehicle was black and shiny with a lot of polished chrome. The supervisor needed its size for his size. Marquise always took the new men to their corner the first time and explained to them as he drove why that corner was chosen for their expansion plans.

After seeing the corner, Marquise told Mo he should be there the next morning. One of the Zombies runners would bring the dope. If a young kid got caught with a substantial amount of crack or H it wouldn't be as bad as if an adult did. A minor would get a slap on the wrist.

Before they got back in the shiny truck, Mo said, "Why don't I walk back? I could use the exercise."

He needed the time alone to text the other detectives and let them know what was happening.

"Suit yourself," said Marquise.

The day was sunny but chilly, unusual for New York in December. Usually it was gloomy and gray. As he walked he sent a group text to Maloney and Musso, giving them the news about his promotion. He would have liked to include his best friend, Jun, but he didn't want to risk compromising him in any way in the event someone else heard the alert and saw the text. The sensitive Filipino's feelings would be hurt but he'd get over it. For a macho Asian and a cop, Jun was pretty sensitive. But only Mo knew it and he'd never let on to anyone else.

***

Cody Hendricks from Nashville, TN, and a University of Tennessee grad, had been in Moscow on business for close to a month, selling farm equipment. The major crops in Russia were wheat, barley, rye, sunflower and potatoes. Interesting, because potatoes weren't harvested for eating but primarily for the manufacturing of vodka, Russia's most popular alcoholic drink. The main staple, because without it, the populace would be unable to survive the harsh Russian winters. Whether that was physical or psychological, or even true, no one knew for sure, but no one was willing to test the theory to find out.

Hendricks was late boarding the KLM 747 flight to Kennedy International. As a reminder of his Tennessee roots, he wore a cream-colored felt cowboy hat and earbuds under the brim so he could listen to the Nashville country he preferred. He thought the Russians liked his look, making them realize they were working with a *real* American. He couldn't get into the newer generation Texas country.

They were unable to accommodate Cody with his usual business-class seat, first-row bulkhead next to one of the restrooms, that so comfortably suited his larger than average size, already given away due to his lateness. He had been a first team All-SEC linebacker for the Vols. Hendricks had been delayed due to a farewell party his hosts, the Russian Department of Agriculture, had thrown in his honor. He'd imbibed in too much good Russian vodka—although he thought that Tito's, made in Austin Texas, was just as good if not better than its Russian counterparts—and now had to pay the price for having too much fun and being late. He wished his Russian hosts hadn't insisted he have one more and one more after that. Then they had a car and driver deliver him to the airport. A big black Zil, an abbreviation for Zavod imeni Likhachova, a classic luxury car not even manufactured any longer, but because it was large and comfortable, it was still used by politicians and for chauffeuring visiting dignitaries. And although most Russians were proud of the railway system, it was way more comfortable than taking the train would have been.

He had to sit mid plane and entered the doorway just behind first class, in front of his usual bulkhead seat

At least the Russians weren't like the British on his last trip to the UK. The Russians had been professional but little more. The British had been so fucking polite—even if they were telling you no, or that they couldn't help you—that it had just annoyed the shit out of him. Although searching his soul, he couldn't figure out why exactly, it had bothered him so. Also, you could disagree about football—soccer in their country—or politics, or the weather, and five minutes later they would be buying you pints, especially after they picked up on on the American accent.

Ducked as he entered the doorway just behind first class and in front of others occupying the usual business class bulkhead seat he considered his.

A flight attendant appearing to be half Asian, approached him. "May I see your boarding pass, sir?"

Checking the seat number and finding everything in order, she turned and said, "Follow me, please."

He liked the way her wavy brown hair swung when she turned, and how her feminine hips moved from side to side as she walked. The one thing that Cody thought made international travel bearable, was that he thought the flight attendants were way hotter than the ones on domestic flights. And since his Chinese girlfriend had just broken up with him he was on the lookout for another Asian.

The flight attendant led him to his seat.

As he made his way he received a couple of hard stares from men, that had he encountered them in a Moscow alley would have caused him to elevate his alert level to condition orange. His senses of intuition and situational awareness were honed from his service in the U.S. Army's Special Forces, commonly known as the Green Berets. He'd noticed five such men spread out over ten rows, who although they didn't sit together gave him the distinct impression that they not only knew each other but were together and pretending not to be. Rough men who looked as though they were hoping for a fight, what they lived for. He could give them one—he had a reputation to protect because in addition to his own Special Forces status his father had been CIA. He wouldn't tarnish the family name.

Hendricks hoped they weren't up to no good because if they were, and if they were any good at what they did—and he guessed they were—they'd sense what he was just as he had them, and target him to be taken out first. And even though he was ex-Army and Special Forces, and used to physical contact from playing SEC football he wouldn't want to be their first target, so Hendricks was glad he was on a large jet with three or four hundred other passengers. Safety in numbers. He decided since he'd been drinking he might as well continue, and should probably stick with vodka. Fortunately, at six-foot-three and a muscular two hundred thirty pounds, the alcohol didn't affect him too much. Soon settled, he ordered a bone-dry martini, almost straight vodka, with three blue cheese–stuffed olives skewered on a blue plastic spear.

He had sucked the bottom out of the cocktail before the plane backed away from the gate and was asleep with it still on the taxiway. He'd developed the ability to fall asleep quickly and sleep anywhere, since in the army you were trained to sleep and eat whenever you could because you didn't know when you would get the chance to do either again. The army agreed with the Jason Bourne axiom from the Robert Ludlum novels, *sleep is a weapon.*

Yet, this time, Hendricks napped restlessly. And dreamed, his brain unable to relax. In his dream he was convinced by someone, or something, not to worry about the rough-looking Russians. To just forget about them. And that's what he did.

When he awoke he thought he was being yelled at by a Special Forces training officer but he was awakened by noise when an elderly couple sitting in the row in front of him, appearing to be middle eastern—Indian or perhaps Pakistani—so, although he spoke passable German, he couldn't understand a word of their language, but from her tone and volume, and the old man's submissive posture, he could guess that the little old woman was giving the man holy hell about something. The old man's tired eyes wore a veil of what-happeneds and what-could-have-beens. Cody wondered how long she'd been doing it and how long ago he'd accepted it as his fate in life. But in his eyes Cody could see a younger man who couldn't comprehend how he'd reached this place.

Gathering his senses, and accessing the video display of the jet's path on the screen in the seatback in front of him, with a waggle of the empty glass, and a nod toward the flight attendant, this one middle-eastern, he ordered another martini. Happy to be serving such a handsome passenger, she cheerfully returned with the cocktail a moment later, but a few minutes after, due to unexpected turbulence that caused him to spill almost half, he was unable to finish it.

"Goddammit," Hendricks said slurring his words slightly, as he used a napkin to blot the wet spots on his western style shirt and the top of his Wrangler jeans. "Fucking rough air." He settled in and over the next few hours followed the large aircraft's path as it traversed Russia, eastern Europe, the UK and an arcing sweep of the Atlantic before entering Laguardia's flight path entering Long Island Sound, nearing the water's surface the closer they got to the pier on which the runway was built. He'd flown that path into LaGuardia quite a few times and still wasn't comfortable with the plane getting nearer and nearer to the water's surface until finally hearing the welcome sound of the landing gear touching down on the runway supported by pilings, that extended into the shallow bay.

As fortune would have it, the rough men had drawn the attention of CIA field officers stationed in Moscow as well. After determining they were en route to America's highest profile city, they notified the NYPD's CIA liaison and by the time the plane touched down on

American soil, Lieutenant Shapiro was expecting some of Russia's most disreputable citizens.

Lt. Shapiro stuck his head only, through the door to yell, "Musso, Maloney…front and center!"

"Yeah, Lou. What's up?"

"Looks like the Russians are bringing in reinforcements."

"Get the fuck outta here," Musso said.

"No, that's what we need to tell *them*," said Maloney, his tongue firmly planted in his cheek.

"All right, get serious, you two. This is no time for B.S. It sounds like we've got trouble coming our way."

Finally turning serious, Musso asked, "Okay boss, what's happening?"

The CIA Chief of Station in Moscow notified us they had five bad guys on a flight from Domodedovo International to JFK yesterday. Ten-hour direct flight means they're already here. They checked flight manifests for the next few days and they've identified at least forty-two known persons of er, ah…let's call it questionable backgrounds.

"We need to alert Hernandez and Louis." Musso said. "Don't want them blind-sided by anything." They were the first ones he thought of and it was the first time he hadn't referred to them as *the kids*.

Maloney agreed. "Especially since Mo's got his own corner, working by himself now."

Shapiro said, "I'll put everybody on this if I need to. Just keep me up to date."

As they exited the lieutenant's office, Musso said, "And you should probably call your asshole buddy. Find out what he knows about this."

Maloney just shook his head at his partner. Already ignoring him, he spoke into the iPhone: "Yeah, De, Detective Maloney. We need to see you again. Sooner rather than later. Yeah I know, I know we just saw you Saturday, but this is pretty big. Okay, good, good. See you then." DeAngelo disconnected the call without replying.

"He'll meet us at the Kentucky Fried at the corner of 169th and Prospect at 5:30."

"He probably wants you to buy him supper. I told you, you were starting something by taking him breakfast."

"Hey, if he can help us head off a drug war I'll buy him a goddamn steak dinner at Peter Luger's," the steakhouse most people considered the best in Manhattan, which most likely made it the best in the world.

'I hear you buddy, but I'm just saying, I think you've started something."

They passed, next door to the restaurant, in a large dirty window, a neon sign announcing a combination massage studio and nail salon. Chinese and Vietnamese working side by side. A Vietnamese Christian church was upstairs. Each side of the door to the KFC was decorated with hand-lettered signs taped to the glass announcing neighborhood dances, one for Latinos and one for Asians, both at the Bronx National Guard Armory on consecutive Saturday nights in January. The chain restaurant had a line of customers placing orders to carry home, but the dining room was empty except for the tall man, who was in a booth and already involved in his meal—two pieces, a leg and thigh, looked like original recipe with a side of mashed potatoes and gravy, cole slaw, a biscuit, a chocolate chip cookie and a Pepsi.

"I got the $5.00 Fillup," De said.

"Looks good," said Maloney.

"It is. I prefer the original recipe. I call it the greasy recipe. Sometimes you just need a lube job, you know."

"Sometimes," agreed Maloney.

"Course I wish I could get one of those cute girls behind the counter to throw in a chicken pot pie gratis. They make 'em just like my grandma used to. I guess I'm not handsome enough, or charming enough, or something. I keep trying, but it just hasn't worked, so far. But…I won't give up."

Musso, impressed that DeAngelo knew the meaning of the word gratis, but also bored listening to his pratter, wandered away and got him and his partner each a Diet Pepsis.

"Sit," said DeAngelo, not unkindly.

Sitting across from DeAngelo in the hard red Formica booth it occurred to Maloney if they'd had a fourth, they'd have looked like the stars of Seinfeld sitting in their favorite booth at Monk's Diner, not far away on Manhattan's Upper West Side, or at least the real diner, Tom's, on which Monk's was based.

"We've heard something new," Musso said, "and we wanted to run it by you.

"Aiight."

"Shit," Musso said, already running out of patience with DeAngelo and his *"aiights."* "He's just doing that to piss me off. Do you want to continue, Detective Maloney?"

"Okay," he said, giving his partner a hard look of frustration. "De, the CIA have tracked five known Russian criminals on a plane to Kennedy. They're already here and they believe even more are on the way."

"Shit," DeAngelo said during a pause in his chewing to dab properly at the corners of his mouth with a napkin wearing the restaurant's trademark red logo. He appeared stunned by the news. After taking a moment to recover, he said, "I'm sorry, dudes, but I've gotta leave."

Not the reaction they'd expected. Maloney said, "Stay in touch, De."

DeAngelo waved off the detective dismissively as he grabbed a New York Knicks jacket from the back of a nearby baby's highchair and left in a rush.

"That was interesting," said Musso.

"Yeah."

Maloney was deep in thought as he watched the tall black man join the throngs on the crowded sidewalk, most of whom were moving with less energy than they'd had when they trekked to work in the morning.

***

Rev had called another meeting with his inner circle. The expression on his face dire, the appearance of a man who'd just lost his mom, his favorite dog and his wife, all in the same week. A brother living life in a country song.

Rev got straight to business. "I have it on good authority the Russians are getting reinforcements from their homeland and I'm more concerned than ever that they are planning war on us. Carmelito, this is your purview, so you should begin preparations."

"Will do, boss. To begin with, I think we should increase the guard presence here on Valentine, immediately."

"Good idea."

"I'll work out other details and have an outline for you within the hour."

"Good, we don't have time to waste. I've gotten word that some of their help have already landed at Kennedy and way more are in transit."

"Damn," said Marquise.

"Yeah. And Marquise, you should probably work with Carmelito. It's your guys out on the street.

Marquise glanced at the man he called Harry and received a slight nod. "On it, boss," he said.

Thinking of all angles, Rev said, "LT, I'm sure these men aren't traveling on legal docs. Is there anything you can do to delay them getting through customs? Make their lives a little more difficult or to keep them from getting here altogether?"

"I've got an old law school classmate who works with the US Marshal's Service. He looks the other way when it comes to what I do. I'll check with him. They probably don't want any more Russian assholes in our country, either."

Rev grinned: "Maybe we can do the US Marshals a favor, curry some good will." That would be ironic—a drug kingpin helping the feds.

"That'd be a trip, wouldn't it," said LT.

"Darelle, you work with LT. Give him any support he needs. Financial, travel help, an ear, anything."

"Whatever you say, boss."

***

As they returned to the cruiser, "I don't know," Maloney said. "I just have an idea that maybe DeAngelo isn't what he says he is."

Musso nodded in agreement. "I'm beginning to think the same thing, but what? Someone in the Zombies, one of the main guys? Why would he turn snitch?"

"I don't know, but if you think about it we've given him more than he's given us."

"Bingo," Musso said. "That's why I didn't like the guy right off the bat. I think we're being played."

Maloney said, "So what do you think? Is he with another agency? Is he a Zombie? One of the big shots? Is he connected to them? What's his agenda?"

"I think," said Musso, "he's one of the head man's higher-ups working on direct orders from the man or—now hear me out—he's the head man himself."

"You're shittin' me. You think DeAngelo's the Rev?"

"I shit you not. And his agenda is to keep up with us, find out what we know. Think about it. It makes sense."

"I don't know, partner. Do you know how that sounds?"

"I know, I know. Sounds crazy, but it's crazy smart. And it would explain a lot. Think about it. He seems more intelligent, more educated, than your average street thug. He likes the Hall of Fame. His clothes are washed. In fact, he smells better than Serpico did when he was undercover."

'You knew Serpico?"

'No, but I heard stories. They say that guy stunk to high Heaven. Said he looked and smelled like his clothes had been pulled out of a camel's ass. But let's stay on point. Except when he's saying *aiight* and *sup,* he speaks well and I just think the street lingo, and all that crap, just might be an act."

"I'm starting to think you might be onto something, Rock, but I'm thinking more along the lines of him being a Fed, working us." That would still follow what you're saying—intelligent, educated, articulate.

" If that's so, the question is who is he, who does he work for, and how do we find out?"

Johnny, always thinking of the new guys said, "One thing's for sure, we need to let Hernandez and Louis know what we're thinking. Don't want them to be caught with their pants down. We need them to be thinking in terms of this, and besides, if they've met the head guy they know what he looks like."

"Yeah, but I know they would have told us if they'd seen the main man or if they even thought they had."

"Yeah, I think so, too. But now more so than ever, they need to keep their eyes open."

"We should also get Buchman to draw him from our scripts."

"Definitely. Let's go see him now."

They called Officer Joseph Buchman "Cowboy Joe" because he was a Dallas Cowboys fan, and they liked him even if he was one. In fact, he liked to wear what looked like cowboy boots, but what no one knew was that even though they had western stitching on the pointed toe and a western heel, they only came up to the ankle, something no self-respecting westerner would be caught dead in.

The inhumanity, a native New Yorker, a Bronxite, a fan of the enemy, in the same division as the Giants, no less. He was forty, rail-thin with black horn-rimmed glasses and reminded one of a younger Woody Allen.

They entered what he called his "studio", just an office with a door that closed, and noted everything was normal: paint, brushes, pens, chalk and paper covering every surface. "Cowboy, how ya' doin?"

He shook his head. "Uh-oh. You hotshots don't usually grace me unless you need something."

Musso said, "And this time is no different. But at least we're consistent."

Maloney shook his head. He would have at least made a little small talk to try and gain some favor.

Disregarding his partner's lack of tact, he said, "Cowboy, listen, we have a snitch and we don't think he's what he says he is, so we need you to draw him from our description, so we can run it through the database of Knowns."

"I can do that. When do you want to do it?"

Musso said, "Five minutes ago."

"Clear those two chairs, then, and let's get to it."

They each emptied armloads of sketches from matching wingback chairs covered in burgundy crushed velvet worn to pale pink in the seats. Once seated, they were distracted by a small flatscreen television in the corner tuned to a rerun of Three's Company. Before they could make a smartass comment, Cowboy said, "I only have it on for background noise. Unless something like 9/11 goes down, and then I'll know about it immediately. Is he white or black?"

Musso waved off the TV and said, "No explanation is necessary.?"

Buchman rescued a spiral-bound pad from under the avalanche of detritus covering his combination desk-drawing table. As he reached for his pastels, Musso said, "Our dude's black." Which prompted the artist to retrieve a couple of small pieces of charcoal from a tray hanging under the desk.

Buchman then collected a Mountain Dew from a small refrigerator on the other side of the room.

"Want one?" he said.

"No, thanks," Maloney replied.

'I'll have a Pepsi if you've got one," said Musso.

"Sorry, bro, All I've got is a case of Dew." He opened the small refrigerator wide so they could see.

Musso and Maloney both looked at him like "have you lost your mind?"

"What can I say? I'm the president and founder of the MD Club—New York City Chapter. I drink 'em for the rush. The highest caffeine soda I can find since Jolt went belly-up. They help with my creativity."

Using their powers of deduction they could tell he'd rehearsed—and used that routine before—probably whenever he opened his fridge in front of anyone who then noticed the large number of green cans.

They all agreed that both detectives would describe what came to mind, and if either could help the other remember, they'd agree on the combined remembrance unless neither could convince the other that their recollection was inaccurate. A few minutes later, Cowboy clunked the empty Mountain Dew can into a small waste basket by the desk, where it came to a rest against three others.

"Grab me another?" He asked Maloney nodding toward the small fridge. Maloney retrieved the soda.

Cowboy shrugged.

"Like I said, I only drink them for the caffeine."

He continued to draw until he finished the can. Maloney noticed and said, "Need another one?"

Cowboy said, "No, I really don't like 'em," and grinned sheepishly.

After most of an hour, Buchman displayed the first draft of the artwork.

Maloney said, "Close, but his nose is thinner."

Musso agreed and then said, "And his neck is more muscular. He looks like an athlete, or like he used to be one, anyway."

Maloney nodded his agreement.

Once the artist patiently made the changes, erasing some of the nose and shading the neck to give the look of more muscle, Musso said, "Perfect! Cowboy, you're a genius."

Maloney said, "Yep, that's him."

Buchman ripped the sheet from the pad and thrust it at Maloney. The detective inferred from that action that the artist had other things to do and it was his way of inviting them to be on their way.

"Thanks, dude," said Maloney.

"Yeah, thanks, bro" said Musso. Then to Maloney, "Let's get it scanned."

"I was ahead of you, Rock."

They went to Musso's Macintosh he'd acquired after a bust in which the bad guy's office equipment was impounded by the department. It was one of the perks of being the senior detective in the Bronx. It had apparently been new when the police confiscated it, because even after Musso's use, the keyboard was still clean, unstained by dirt. Using an HP scanner, the drawing was entered and in a minute they were running it against their database of known bad guys.

It took longer than an hour to run the image against the photos of thousands of BGs, and when the screen flashed COMPLETE, without a hit, Musso said, "Shit. Nothing."

"The guy doesn't have a record? That's impossible," said Maloney.

"Okay. We have to do this the hard way. Make copies and get 'em on the street."

Musso said, "That'll be a good job for some rookie unis."

"Lou'll get 'em for us."

Using Musso's scanner/printer again, the detectives made an eight by ten poster of the drawing with the words "Call if you recognize this man" and a phone number. They set the printer for a thousand copies. The phone number was to a switchboard that was manned by volunteer soft spoken retired women twenty-four/seven. The department didn't want a rough-sounding, masculine voice to scare anyone off.

Lt. Shapiro got the loan of a dozen young uniform officers to tape the posters on light poles and telephone poles populating the south Bronx.

"So, you know what to do. Put one on every utility pole north and east of the Harlem River until you run out of posters. You've got a thousand; that's roughly eighty-five a piece. You go getters can take care of that in no time. Now get out there."

There was some under-their-breath grumbling but they were rookie patrol officers and they had to do whatever was asked of them. They would get it done and be back in a few hours.

"What do you think is gonna happen?" Musso asked.

"I hope a well-meaning citizen recognizes him, even if they don't know him, thinks he's missing and believing they're being helpful, gives us a call."

"That's how I'm hoping it plays out."

Musso sighed as he stood and said, "I'm going to call it a day."

Maloney said, "Sounds like a good idea."

It had been a long day and now they hoped they would find out just who DeAngelo really was. Neither felt like going to the Pound.

"See you in the morning."

"Yeah, Rock, see you in the a.m."

***

Before they finished a single cup of crappy break-room coffee, Maloney said, "All right, let's do it. I waited until you got here because I'm nervous about it, but let's see if we got any calls."

Musso said, "Sounds like a plan. I can't drink anymore of this shit anyways," and poured his cup of swill in the sink, then turned and made a soft jump shot with the wadded-up paper cup into a nearby wastebasket.

Maude, who was just starting the morning shift, nodded as they approached her desk and said, "Good morning, detectives."

"Good morning, m'lady," Maloney responded. He could charm women of any age: Two to ninety-two. And this one was closer to the upper end of that range. She smiled and if a woman her age was capable of it, blushed.

"Mornin'," said Musso. He didn't care how he sounded.

Maloney asked, "Did we get any calls on our poster?"

Maude said, "The overnight lady didn't leave me a note, and she would've if we had."

"Damn," Musso muttered.

Maloney said, "Come on, Rocky, we really didn't expect to hear anything the first day."

"You're right, I didn't expect it, but I could hope."

"I know. I hoped, too. But we gotta be realistic.'

As they turned and left Maude's small office, Shapiro approached them. "Rock, Maloney, glad I found you. Just heard from our CIA liaison. They picked up eight Russian assholes at JFK yesterday."

"Get the fuck outta here," Musso said, cheerfully.

Maloney said, "How?"

"US Marshals' Service called them. Apparently *they* received an anonymous tip. The CIA staked out baggage claim and bingo, eight Ivans in custody. At least it's good to know federal agencies are communicating with each other. But, I have to run to a meeting. Keep me informed."

As Shapiro made his exit, Musso said, "Yeah, Lou's right. It's a lot better than pre-9/11. The alphabet agencies didn't communicate at all back then." He continued. " Hmm, an anonymous tip. Now who could have given them that?"

Maloney said, "Who indeed?"

"We tell your buddy, De, about it and next thing you know, eight Russians are cuffed at Kennedy. How could that happen?"

"The plot thickens," said Maloney.

"I think this is a good indication that he isn't what he pretends to be."

"Agreed, partner. But here's another thought. What if he's with one of the big agencies?"

"You mean a Fed?"

"Why not? Anything's possible. Someone—I don't remember who—once said *if you eliminate the obvious and all that's left is the ridiculous, then that's the answer. No matter how ridiculous.* We haven't eliminated anything about him yet, so I think we have to consider everything. "

"You know, I would never have thought that. But this is turning weird, so I won't discount anything. That means when he gets out of his meeting we should tell Lou what we're thinking just in case there are Feds involved."

"Yeah, he can probably find it out if that's what's going on."

If Musso felt like they should tell the lieutenant, it was even more worrisome to Maloney since his partner usually preferred doing things on his own, without outside interference.

"Yeah, he can probably find out if that's what's happening"

***

Nobody could remember seeing Arkady like this. Way beyond being pissed. His face was twisted into a mask of blood red rage.

"Goddammit! We lost eight soldiers and if the fucking CIA can stop them, then it means they can stop the others that are on the way. Fuck."

***

LT sat in front of Rev's desk.

"What you got for me?" Rev was intensely focused on the Russians.

"My friend at the Marshals Service said they arrested eight Russians yesterday."

"Good job, LT."

"Thanks boss. Just doing my job."

Rev felt like the best thing he did was hire good people. LT was proof of that. And he knew the others in his inner circle were just as good and dedicated. Would do anything for him.

***

Mo was on his corner early and a runner—an ambitious kid who'd proven himself trustworthy enough to deliver the stuff—showed up five minutes later with the merch and a roll of fives and tens for change. The cold weather was schizophrenic; dark clouds and light ones in ferocious battle for ownership of the sun. The runner left and Mo wrapped his hands around a large cup of coffee, trying to stave off the chill. He inhaled its warmth deeply.

Working by himself, Louis had a little privacy, so he texted Maloney to check-in. Maloney replied to the text and told him about his and Musso's suspicions.

Mo texted again, "Yeah, I saw some of those posters on my walk north this morning." His South Bronx apartment was almost in the center of the grid where the rookie uniforms were putting up the notices the previous day.

Maloney replied, "You didn't see them yesterday afternoon?"

"Had a date; got home late. Didn't notice them in the dark."

"I guess you need a life."

"Thanks. But if you don't have one I probably don't need one either. We're supposed to be married to the job anyway, aren't we?"

Maloney didn't know what to make of the young detective giving him the business except to reply, "Touché."

Then, "Anyway, Rocky and I wanted you and Hernandez to know what's going on; it's more important than ever for you guys to be alert."

Detective Louis sent one last text. "Just remember, Jun still has somebody watching his every move, so don't text him."

"I remember. Whoever sees him first, tell him face to face."

With all the texting Louis was doing his coffee had gone cold. He walked to the street curb, squatted and poured what remained into the gutter.

***

Hernandez and Louis arrived back at Ft. Apache at almost the same time Musso and Maloney were leaving.

Maloney said, "Glad we ran into you guys. How about a cold one?"

Hernandez said, "Only one?"

Louis said, "That's what I was wondering." The rookie detectives were learning.

Musso said, "We'll be there. You just better get there soon or we'll drink it all."

Hernandez said, "They don't have San Mig, the national beer of the Philippines. So it won't be any big loss if you do.

Musso, working on his smart-assery, replied. "Okay, I'm just saying." It didn't fit him.

"Give us five," said Louis. "And there better be some Gun Hill left," knowing he and Musso both drank the local Bronx microbrew. Maloney grinned, seeing how the kids were learning to dish it out. Especially at his partner's expense. Musso just looked surprised.

***

The bell over the door to the Pound jingled. Brendan saw that two of his best customers were entering.

He welcomed them warmly. "Rock, John, where youse guys been?"

Maloney said, "Ah, you know ups and downs of the job."

Musso: "Busier than a one-legged man in an ass-kicking contest."

"I hear ya. Just glad youse are back."

"Thanks. Glad to be back," said John.

"Ditto," Rock added.

***

Maude caught Maloney as he entered the precinct. Holding aloft several pink slips of paper, she said, "Detective, we got some calls overnight, about your poster."

"Great," he said as he practically yanked them from her tiny, frail hands and thumbed through them. They all read a variation of the same theme: *Don't have a name... A homeless man, wandering aimlessly. Will let you know if we see him again.* The good news was none of them sounded like crazies—which was good. Asking the public for help always brought the whack jobs out of the woodwork. At least this time no one saw him getting out of a spaceship or wearing a tutu while riding a pink elephant down Valentine.

"Damn," he said, then, "Sorry." He felt bad about swearing in front of the kindly old lady.

"No, I'm sorry," said Maude, "sorry that it wasn't what you hoped." She sounded like she was sincere.

Disappointed, Maloney barely made it up the stairs. Beaten. His enthusiasm was dampened. The energy of the bright new morning drained. Musso said, "You look like somebody ran over your cat."

"We got four hits off our poster, but everyone said the same thing: An unknown homeless guy."

"Shit. Thanks for raining on my parade."

"Misery loves company, partner."

***

"Our CIA liaison reports they've arrested twenty-seven Russian thugs in the last week and a half," Maloney reported to his partner. "But it seems like their arrivals were slowing down anyways. Like maybe their reason for coming is close."

"And less than a week before Christmas," Musso said, "You don't think those sons of bitches are looking to fuck up Christmas, do youse?"

"Terrorists do it. I wouldn't put it past these sons of bitches, either. We have to be ready for that, Rock."

. "Yeah, Rock. I second that. Shapiro agreed. "I'm cancelling Christmas off-time. Hate to do it. Knowing everyone's probably made their holiday plans, but we've gotta be prepared. So, it's all hands on deck until we see what's up. In fact, I'll call your buddies at ESU. If the shit-hits-the-fan I'd like to have them on stand by to help with the heavy lifting."

"That's a real smart idea, Lou. I'd feel better, knowing we have them ready."

The lieutenant really didn't want to mess up anybody's Christmas, but he had to consider the well being of the people of New York before anything else.

Chapter Thirteen
Silent Night, Deadly Night

A dynamic speaker, Arkady's men were a rapt audience, as he challengingly eyed then and spoke.

"Our time approaches," Arkady said, "Mere days before we strike on the eve of the birth of their king. We have lost most of the reinforcements we were expecting from the glorious motherland, but no matter. We will rain down hell on them without the help of our comrades."

***

Christmas was a little more than seventy-two hours away and Jun was feeling ill. He needed to find the perfect engagement ring for his Anne, and make it seem like he'd had it planned for weeks and that it wasn't a last-minute decision. He and Mo met at Fort Apache for coffee before going to their corners.

"Dude, I need some help," he said to his friend.

"I'm here for you brother. Whatchu need?"

"You don't know anything about diamonds, do you?"

"Whatchu think?" His partner said, twirling one of his diamond stud earrings between his thumb and forefinger.

"I'm serious, bruv. I got three days to find an engagement ring for Anne."

Mo took a long draw from his cup then said, "Not to worry. I know a guy."

Jun held up his hands palms out. "No, no, Mo. This can't be one of your fly-by-night street dealers. I need a first-class diamond. This is for the love of my life."

"No, man," Mo protested. "This is a Jewish gentleman in the diamond district. A friend of my father's from back in the day, back when he walked a beat. He'll hook you up, no sweat. He always said he'd give me a brother-in-law deal on a ring, but since I don't have any solid prospects and me and you are brothers from different mothers, I'll pass my deal to you. How's that sound?"

Jun leaned across the cheap Formica-topped table, hugged his best friend and said, "That sounds too good to be true."

"So meet me back here at the end of the day and I'll take you to see him."

"Awesome! You're saving my life, dude."

"Come on, man. What're brothers for?" They downed their cups, fist-bumped and went their separate ways.

***

After meeting at the precinct, Mo and Jun walked to the nearby south Bronx train station and after boarding, twenty-two minutes later and four dollars lighter, they entered Grand Central Station. Signaling one of the waiting cabs, yellow though it was, and smelling of burning incense with wooden beads hanging from the rear view mirror, that was as close as it got to a typical large four door New York taxi, a diminutive Toyota hatchback, a hybrid no less, a five minute ride later and they were waiting to to be buzzed into Mr. Abramowitz's jewelry showroom. Mo had to peer through the glass door until he was recognized, since like all jewelers in the district they kept the doors locked. Once he was, they were buzzed into the black carpeted medium-sized room with six long glasses cases running from the front to the rear of the store. After a young lady locked the door behind them, Mr. Abramowitz exited his office to greet Mo with a big bearhug. He wore a black brimmed hat, had the long curly sideburns of a Hasidic Jew, a long beard and wore a loupe over his right eye, with which to examine stones. The typical uniform of a Hasidic Jewish diamond merchant, black polyester pants, a white short-sleeved shirt and black tie.

"Morris, my boy, how are you?"

"Just fine, Papa, just fine. This is my friend, Tony—we call him Jun. He needs an engagement ring."

"It's nice to meet you, young man. And congratulations. You've come to the right place."

"Thank you, sir. That's what I hear. And it's nice to meet you, sir."

"How can I help you? Do you know what you want?"

"Sir, I'd like the highest quality, biggest diamond I can get for no more than fifteen thousand dollars—ah… and the closer to ten, the better. But I need your guidance. I've never done this before."

Mo's eyes got unnaturally big when his friend mentioned those, what were to him astronomical numbers.

Jun shrugged and said, "What can I say? I've been saving up."

Filipinos were known for being frugal and like most Asians didn't often use credit cards, preferring to use cash whenever possible.

"Fine, just fine. I'm sure we can find something suitable. Walk this way, please. This case contains stones in that range." Abramowitz gestured to the first row nearest the entrance, to draw customers' attention and pulled out a beautiful, royal cut, one-and-a-third carat diamond. He said, "This one is near-perfect in cut, clarity and color and the carat weight is substantial. It's a beautiful stone in all ways."

"It is beautiful. How much is it?"Anxious to get a ring for Anne, Jun was ready to pull the metaphorical trigger.

"For my Godson's best friend, eleven thousand dollars in the white gold ring and setting of your choice. But let's look at some others before you make up your mind."

Abramowitz showed him a half-dozen other stones, all beautiful, but nearly two hours later Jun returned to the first. He gazed at it, imagining it on Anne's perfectly graceful finger and said, "This is the one."

Jun picked out a beautiful slim white gold band and he was ready. Mr. Abramowitz placed it in the setting and mounted it while they waited.

The kindly Jewish gentleman even gave him interest-free terms. Said, "My wedding present to my Godson's friend."

"Thank you, sir. I'm very grateful."

Mo said, "Yes, Papa, thank you."

"Give your daddy my love." Abramowitz respected Mo's father, Henry, and loved him as if he were a younger brother.

"I will, Papa.

"And don't be a stranger, my son. What are you, too busy to visit your papa?"

"No, Papa. I'll be back.

Back on the sidewalk, still ecstatic about his purchase, Jun said, "What a sweet old man."

"I told you," said Mo.

Indeed, he had.

***

The Bronx City Courthouse was on 161st street, about a mile and a half from Fort Apache. Detective Maloney decided to hoof it. He had to make an appearance in the Gerald Whitman case but he didn't feel good about it. Corner dealers were the low men on the totem pole and until they arrested some of the Zombies' higher-ups they weren't doing any real damage. With an almost unlimited supply of undereducated young men interested in earning easy money, the gang could easily replace any arrested dealers—all of whom were expendable.

The court appearance went as expected. The evidence was overwhelming and with the testimony of a respected NYPD detective, open and shut. In and out in thirty minutes. Gerald got fifteen years. Maloney saw tears pooling in the kid's eyes when the verdict was read.

What Maloney didn't notice was the large African-American man sitting in the back row. Rev obviously couldn't show up, so Marquise was his representative. And he felt sorry for Gerald's family. A big, but emotional man, nascent tears were starting to form, so he slipped out before anyone would notice.

He dialed Rev. "He's gone, boss, fifteen big ones."

"Damn," said Rev and clicked off. Inconsolable, he felt like he was to blame. He'd had other dealers who'd been arrested before, but this one was different.

***

Maloney completed his paperwork and turned it in. Then went to commiserate with Musso. Partners for ten years, he now needed the friendship part of the relationship. It had been an emotional morning for him, causing him to wonder if he still had the cajones for the job— this part of it, anyway.

Leaning against Musso's desk, Maloney said, "Rock, I don't know. I just don't know if I have the stomach for it anymore. Arresting kids that should be in school. Most of them just trying to earn enough money to buy some new Air Jordans, or help a broken family put food on the table. We send them away and they come back middle-aged men, beaten down, hardened criminals. I just don't know if I can do this anymore. I need to hurry up and finish school. Get my law degree. Hell, I might have gotten that kid off, or at least gotten him a shorter sentence. I don't take any pride in arresting kids. I want the head man, the one they call Rev."

"You're dreaming, man. Rev's a ghost. Nobody knows him. I'm not even sure I believe he's real; I think he might be a myth."

"Maybe you're right, Rock. But I need to get a serious bust to hurt the Zombies, not this penny-ante shit."

"I hear you, brother."

"What's even worse is I feel like Rev is mocking us, laughing at us. Some nights when I'm asleep I hear him in my dreams…and they become nightmares."

***

Christmas Eve afternoon: In their warehouse headquarters, Arkady was firing up the troops. He gave them a pep talk, mostly explaining that he would shoot them himself if they didn't take care of business. A pretty motivating pitch.

"Now, go get some rest. Eat and sleep. It will be a long night. We rest until eight pm. We leave at ten. That will get us to the Valentine Street at midnight, the devil's hour. It's how you say—ironic. We attack Valentine on Christmas."

A pair of Russian henchmen took two nondescript, dirty panel trucks that would attract no attention to get fueled up. There could be no hitches. The operation had to run like a finely-tuned Swiss timepiece.

This would be Arkady's finest hour.

***

Christmas Eve afternoon: The drug trade was brisk on Jun's and Mo's corners. Customers purchasing their holiday supply. Would have to last them though the weekend. Wouldn't want the wife and kids to wonder where dad was going if he left the house on Christmas Day.

Jun's mind wasn't on the drug business, though. He was nervous, his anxiety mounting hour by hour, about giving Anne the engagement ring the next day. They'd talked about getting married for months, but this was going to be a total surprise. The ring now safe in his desk drawer, he'd drained his savings.

But would she love it, or even want it? He wouldn't be satisfied unless she thought it was the most beautiful ring she'd ever seen.

***

Rev listened to his gut, and made the same decision that Lieutenant Shapiro had. More men around the Valentine St. headquarters until they knew what was going to happen. At the risk of messing up his men's Christmas, Rev ordered Carmelito to call in the first and second security groups—a total of twenty-four shooters—until the threat passed. He had no idea just how messed up their Christmas would be.

***

Arkady's gunsmiths had fitted the weapons they'd bought from the Romanians with homemade sound suppressors, more commonly known as silencers. They hoped to take down a few Zombies before waking the neighborhood—or at least until the Zombies returned unsuppressed fire.

At 8pm the Russian henchmen were awakened from where they slept, on cots in the rear of the warehouse.

They ate and dressed in silence. No levity, no small talk. This was their pregame prep. In their routine. A couple did pushups. One punched a heavy bag, several, being Catholic, prayed. One said the Rosary. Changed into all black clothes. They would add blackout face paint toward the end of the ride to Valentine Street, thinking it wouldn't be wise to be stopped by cops while wearing blackened faces. As if fifty men in two trucks, carrying assault rifles wouldn't be enough to raise the suspicion of law enforcement.

They piled into the two small size moving vans with engines running at 9:50 pm, and at ten, like clockwork, the warehouse door rose and they departed. They'd allotted two hours from their Brooklyn headquarters to the Bronx, even though it shouldn't take near that long, even if Christmas Eve partiers made the typically bad New York City traffic even crazier. A good thing they did, because it took close to the entire allotted time to get there.

Fortunately the Zombies Valentine Street neighborhood was all but deserted around the brownstone headquarters. Rev had chosen the location because of the relatively sparse population in the two or three blocks north and south of it. And chalking it up to the sounds and bright lights of the noisiest and brightest city in the world, even if the neighbors did hear the trucks it would cause most people to ignore them.

Dressed in tactical all black and their faces now blacked out, the Russians were ready for the assault.The first van parked one-hundred, twenty-five feet north of the house and the second one-hundred, twenty-five feet south of it. Classic battle tactics on the early 1900's, two-story structure that had fewer windows on each end.

From each truck they ran as quickly as possible, weapons ready. An old man bundled up against the frigid Christmas Eve night across the street and a half block down was walking his brindle-colored, pit-bull-boxer mix.

Three days after the start of winter, the old man was bundled up against the frigid Christmas Eve night, as he waited patiently for his equally old dog to pee against the base of a fire hydrant. Hearing the muffled sounds of the Russians, the dog let out a single, quiet bark followed by a low growl. The aged man didn't seem to notice the assault teams. He must have been half-blind and hard of hearing. Two quiet thaps from a suppressed assault weapon dispatched man and dog. Killing one innocent old man and his dog meant nothing to the Russians. The trained killers would not risk being seen or heard this early in the mission.

The team approaching from the north in groups of four as they reached the side of the house, ducked behind a large, loud, heating and air-conditioning unit. The noise from the machine's motor masked the sound of their rustling clothes, scrabble of boots and grunts as they dropped to the ground.

Four men from the south team lay on the cold winter earth below a brick wall defining the back porch. In the kitchen a light flashed on. All four puckered when the rear door of the house opened. A single man emerged but only to answer the call of nature, like an old dog marking his territory. He unzipped as he walked and pissed off the side of the porch into the winter remains of an untended flowerbed that had already received its first blanket of snow. The assault weapon he wore on a sling over his shoulder wouldn't do him any good. The lead man in the group of four, moving quickly and quietly, unsheathed an all black tactical knife, mounted the porch steps and buried the blade in the man's spine where it connected with the head of the unsuspecting Zombie. A spray of hot blood caused by the pressure in the spine of the victim, covered the killer's arm above the elbow and the Zombie died with a small gasp escaping a grimace and a violent surprised look frozen on his face. The Russian dropped the new corpse into the flowerbed where he'd just pissed. A disgraceful end, lying in his own waste, dying because he'd performed a natural bodily function.

As the killer returned and squatted next to his group, the door opened again and a wide-eyed young black man emerged.

"Calvin…Calvin, where'd that brother get off to?" He was only checking on his friend. Shuffling to the end of the porch, he stopped and peered over the railing. The last thing that entered his mind was the image of his dead friend—that and the blunt sensation of a .223 caliber round ripping into his brain.

The element of surprise blown, the Russians burst through the door, and into the kitchen. A small breakfast area, where four Zombies were playing poker and drinking cheap domestic beer. A massacre ensued as suppressed .223 caliber rounds tore through flesh and bone, ripping them apart. The small area's floor quickly was awash with a pool and the coppery stench of blood.

A blur of rushing combatants. Sharp thunder of Zombie weapons, the soft patter of the Russians in return. Cutting streaks of blood. Screams. Curses cut off in mid-sentence. Chaos as the assault teams raced upstairs, other groups racing to the basement. Bodies piling one atop another—Russians as well as Zombies. A bloodbath. In a second floor bedroom, Harry frantically called Rev to let him know, that "the mother-fuckin' Russians" had attacked.

About the time of Harry's call to Rev, equally frantic citizens were dialing 911. The detectives from Fort Apache responded. Musso, the senior detective on duty, shouted to Maloney, Hernandez and Louis, "It's what we've been expecting. We got ourselves a war zone."

***

Harry died wearing midnight-blue silk pajamas, and wielding a 15 round 9mm Walther PPK. Merely descending one step onto the downward staircase and pointing the weapon in the direction of the Russians, brought down a hail of automatic gunfire that literally cut his head from his shoulders. His body fell where it was hit, and, taking a header, his head continuing to fall, rolling down the stairs until it reached the Russian gunmen who coldly kicked the bloody annoyance out of their path. A soccer kick. "Get the fuck out of my way," said one unaffectedly, to what had been Harry's perfectly coiffed head.

***

Musso and the Fort Apache detectives arrived moments before the heavier-armed ESU team only because, their Christmas vacation cancelled, they'd bivouacked at the precinct. Although well-trained and capable, most of the detectives' work was in investigations after the commission of crimes and they didn't mind having the power of the ESU which arrived by helicopter and heavily armored truck. This was the team's usual work and wouldn't even cause a blip in their blood pressure.

The ESU chopper disgorged troops and, after ascending to a safer altitude, shone its spotlight on the structure. The propwash and thunder from its engine was a distracting contribution to the blue-strobe disorientation and confusion, much like that caused by multiple stun grenades, on the scene.

Over the sound of the Zombies' return gunfire, the helicopter's rotor and sirens of other units arriving, the NYPD weren't sure those shooting in the house could hear anything. Even so, the ESU commander grabbed a megaphone and ordered them to stop firing.

Fat chance.

After losing over half their number—twenty-five had been staying there—the remaining Zombies barricaded themselves in a safe room, the one hardened room in the house. The Russians had lost six of their fifty. They were protecting their position in the hallway leading to the safe room, furniture piled atop more furniture as they continued firing at the enemy to no effect.

Hernandez and Louis raced to the sound of the guns–much like firefighters entering a burning building—and directly into the shitstorm through the house's rear entrance.

Maloney said, "Well, fuck," to no one in particular, and followed them into the riotous cacophony of gunfire.

Musso saw his partner and screamed, "Johnny, stop…John…Johnny, no," to no avail. "Shit."

Hernandez and Louis entered the house at the rear and met fire from the few Russians that remained downstairs to cover their upstairs comrades. The young detectives wore body armor, but one of the Russians was firing a .308 caliber assault rifle, which had the power to penetrate most second-chance vests. Hernandez was knocked backward. Louis leaped to his fallen partner, attempting to get cover behind the hard sides of a filled dishwasher. Maloney covered them both with a mean flurry of return fire at the Russians, simultaneously shouting into his Bluetooth mic, "Officer down. Officer down. Kitchen, rear of the house, officer down…"

Mo leaned over his best friend and partner. As he attempted to comfort his friend, Hernandez summoned every ounce of strength and will he could muster to overcome the pain of talking caused by the massive stomach wound. "Everything's dark. Can't see shit. The ring…Mo, the ring is in my desk." Even in death, he nodded to the right, trying to indicate which drawer. Filipinos never spoke or would at the very least, speak less if a nod, a head shake or gesture would suffice. "Give it to Anne…Tell her I loved her before I was born and I'll love her after I die…Tell her…"

A sharp gasp, a spittle of blood. And Hernandez was dead.

***

Before Maloney had time to react to Hernandez's death, a tall African-American man appeared from behind Musso—out of the dark, ghost-like, almost from nowhere—to kneel beside him.

He said, "Sorry, Detective Musso, but I'm going in. Cover me, okay?"

Stunned, Musso said, "DeAngelo, what the hell'er you doing here?"

"I'm going in, Detective." he said. "These are my people. They call me Rev" And with a knowing smile, spun on his heels and with the grace and elegance of an athlete, sprinting at angles, to avoid gunfire, bolted toward the rear of the house.

Rev managed to make the kitchen and return two rounds from his own weapon before he was cut down by a hail of ammo from high-powered Russian gunfire.

Johnny leaped to his feet and shot two Russians, then gingerly stepped to DeAngelo's bloody body.

Stunned, Johnny yelled, "DeAngelo, what the hell is going on?"

The tall man said, "Johnny, I'm Rev." And with his intelligent eyes registering shock and pain at the world of his own making, died. Maloney closed Rev's eyes for him, his own face reflecting sadness. He'd come to respect DeAngelo, even like him, and maybe—just maybe—in a different time or place thought they might have become friends. He'd like to think Rev would feel the same way.

The shooting eventually subsided, the remaining Russians and Zombies rounded up, cuffed and loaded into a transport truck for New York's finest to deliver to New York's boldest—officers from the New York Department of Corrections.

One of the detectives yelled at a uniformed officer. "Youse guys be careful of the cargo. We wouldn't want damaged goods to arrive at the gas chamber." All the officers knew it was a joke, before a trial, charges, or even booking. But it wouldn't hurt anything to put a little scare into the prisoners.

The wounded were carted off to a Bronx Lebanon Hospital Center, and the dead unceremoniously packed into the meat wagon to be delivered to the Bronx county coroner's office in Elmont,

It would be a busy Christmas morning. One they wouldn't soon forget.

***

Christmas day dawned gloomy for the entire city, not just the men and women of Fort Apache, who were mourning the loss of one of their own. Early morning church bells heralded Christ's birth. Detective Morris Louis woke to a gentle rain changing to snow, bringing with it a white Christmas that on any other would be welcome and life affirming.

But not on this day when Mo was going not only as an NYPD detective but also as Jun's best friend to the apartment where, in the Filipino way, Anne lived with her parents, her grandmother—called nanay in Tagalog, the native Filipino language—her younger sister and her mother's sister—called tia, Tagalog, for aunt.

After peeing, brushing his teeth, a shower, and putting on his pants and a t-shirt, he poured some dry food into his Labrador retriever, Norbert's, bowl, patted him on the head and said, "Merry Christmas, Norbert. What're you gonna do while I'm gone? I know what you're gonna do. You're gonna sleep your ass off. Now, you be a good boy." He then shaved and finished dressing.

A uniformed officer answered the door. "Please come in," he said to Detective Louis, not knowing who he was but treating him with the proper respect, nonetheless.

The small apartment was full of somber people. The happy Christmas tree in stark contrast to the intense sadness permeating the room and soaking the papered walls. Musso, Maloney and Lieutenant Shapiro were already there, plus all the other detectives from Fort Apache. The other uniforms, Louis surmised were most likely from Jun's last precinct. One of the uniformed officers holding a wad of cash approached all others, collecting money for Anne. Since she and Jun weren't married she wasn't entitled to any of his benefits. Cops were especially good about taking care of their own and now Anne was one of theirs, forever. A tiny Catholic priest, about five feet tall, who was most likely Filipino, stood nearby offering comfort but not wanting to intrude.

Without speaking, Mo shook hands with Lou, Carmine and John, and learned that Jun's mother, accompanied by her brother, a Monsignor in the Catholic Church, was already on an early morning flight from Ninoy Aquino Airport in Manila, to Kennedy International. Lieutenant Shapiro had made arrangements for two uniformed officers to collect and deliver them to the Bronx apartment. Even though the apartment was small, Anne's family would make room for them. They were now family.

Shapiro, glancing around nervously, said to his detectives, "I need to find the bathroom. I'm gonna be sick." He was turning a sickly shade of mottled green. He'd always had a weak stomach. And this one hit him especially hard. A moment later the muffled sounds of retching through the closed door of the hall bathroom.

Shortly after Mo arrived, the police commissioner made an appearance. On his way to Christmas mass, stricken with emotion, his eyes were red but he looked smart in his dress blues. He grieved for every man or woman lost in the line of duty, and introduced himself to Anne—he obviously'd been briefed on the individuals involved. Squatting in front of her, he took her hands in his and, ignoring all others in the room, they spoke informally for a moment. He would leave for mass at St Nicholas of Tolentine, otherwise known by parishioners and those in the neighborhood as the Cathedral of the Bronx, as soon as this distasteful tragic part of his job was done. Although this was the most difficult part of his position, the commissioner was at his best at times like this—dignified, proper, sensitive and deeply caring. A father to all the city's men and women in blue.

The wonderful aroma of exotic Filipino foods filled the apartment. No telling how long mom, Nanay and Tia had been cooking.

Anne sat on a worn but clean sofa of green chenille with her mother and Nanay on either side. Always slim, she now appeared bone-thin, her eyes listless, yet her heart crying out wanting to comfort her love child, the ultimate Christmas present from her beloved Antonio. She had planned on telling him about the baby on this special day in the Filipino culture, Christmas, her special present for him. But now... he'd never know. Mo approached her and, with the white ring box gingerly balanced on the palm of his hand, went down on one knee, and appearing as if he were the one proposing, his voice breaking, said, "Anne, this is a present from Jun. He wasn't alone. I was with him when he passed. He intended for this to be his Christmas gift for you. With his last words, he told me to make sure I gave it to you. He said he loved you before he was born and he'll love you after he dies."

Grieving, Anne accepted the ring from Mo before the tears flowed and the eruption of sobbing began, no doubt not for the last time. She slumped over onto her grandmother and the older woman supported her.

Stricken with emotion, Mo broke down and sobbed. His body trembled from his heaving. Exhausted from the long Christmas Eve night battling Russians and Zombies and overcome by his own feelings of anguish from losing his best friend and playing this role in Jun and Anne's final chapter, with great effort he rose, but stumbled while getting to his feet. Musso, pretending not to watch, but noticing the scene rushed over to come respectfully to the assistance of the young man.

"Let me help you, Detective."

Thanks, Detective." Detective Louis gracefully responded.

Gripping the ring in her fragile hand, Anne slumped onto her grandmother's shoulder. Christmas would never be the same.

Books by A. Shane Etter

Bottom Dwellers

Mind Dwellers

Trail Dwellers

A Brain in Third Person

Also by A. Shane Etter fromThomasMax Publishing

Pennington Wentworth, II lives in a penthouse condominium in Atlanta and enjoys the finer things in life—expensive wine, the finest restaurants, designer clothes, the best hair salons and the priciest manicures—until he suffers a traumatic brain injury in a car accident.

Then his life changes forever, Atlanta's normally peaceful landscape is equally changed as "Bad Penny" begins his reign of terror. Not since serial killer Wayne Williams terrorized the city while committing the Atlanta Child Murders, has the city been paralyzed with such fear.

With his brain injury apparently permanent he has no recollection of his previous life and moves forward with his plans to become America's all-time, most prolific serial killer. If not for outstanding police work from a joint task force involving detectives of the Atlanta Police Department and those from America's spookiest city, Savannah, GA, he might have been successful. $12.95 for print edition, $4.99 for Kindle or Nook e-book editions.

www.ingramcontent.com/pod-product-compliance
Lightning Source LLC
Chambersburg PA
CBHW022155260626
47155CB00018B/1934